A Candlelight Ecstasy Romance®

"OUR LITTLE AFFAIR IS OVER, DION."

"Do you expect me to believe that, Randi?"

"I don't care what you believe. To get the best out of my actors, I make love to them. Since the series is over, you can take your pretty face elsewhere."

Dion frowned in confusion. "Why are you saying these things? What are you getting at?"

"Don't ask me. You're the one who mixes acting with real life. Was it a coincidence that you pursued me? The similarity of the real and filmed situations is amazing! They say that art mirrors life, but when it's the other way around, there's something wrong."

"This has been building up in you for a long time, hasn't it? You thought I was a royal jerk but you pretended we had a good relationship anyway? To think I respected *your* honesty . . . talk about being real! I'll get out of your life if you want. You're not the only one who feels betrayed."

CANDLELIGHT ECSTASY ROMANCES®

MORE THAN
A DREAM

Lynn Patrick

A CANDLELIGHT ECSTASY ROMANCE®

Published by
Dell Publishing Co., Inc.
1 Dag Hammarskjold Plaza
New York, New York 10017

ISBN: 0-440-15828-1

Printed in the United States of America

First printing—May 1985

For Veronica Mary

To Our Readers:

We have been delighted with your enthusiastic response to Candlelight Ecstasy Romances®, and we thank you for the interest you have shown in this exciting series.

In the upcoming months we will continue to present the distinctive sensuous love stories you have come to expect only from Ecstasy. We look forward to bringing you many more books from your favorite authors and also the very finest work from new authors of contemporary romantic fiction.

As always, we are striving to present the unique, absorbing love stories that you enjoy most—books that are more than ordinary romance. Your suggestions and comments are always welcome. Please write to us at the address below.

Sincerely,

The Editors
Candlelight Romances
1 Dag Hammarskjold Plaza
New York, New York 10017

CHAPTER ONE

The narrow path wound tightly beneath palms, jade trees, pines and other foliage whose lush growth almost blotted out the sky. Gravel crunching beneath her feet, Randi St. Martin strode purposefully, her lightweight jacket slung over one arm, a leather briefcase beneath the other. As the director of the television miniseries *Chrysalis,* she didn't want to be late for the preproduction meeting. Those most important to the success of the program —cinematographer, art director, costume designer, script writer, major stars—would all be there.

Still, it was hard to resist the magic of this familiar place, especially at dusk. For a moment she was exploring an enchanted jungle with blue-green depths holding mysterious secrets, rather than crossing an overgrown garden in Beverly Hills. Hearing the pleasant tinkling of wind chimes, Randi slowed, breathing in the fragrant air.

"Yaah! What the . . . !"

Randi almost jumped out of her skin. "What's wrong? Benny?" She'd thought the producer from Sequoia Productions was right behind her. Retracing her steps, Randi circled a yucca plant and found Benny Fields staring into a veritable forest of spiky bromeliads.

"I thought the damn thing was real!" he yelled, jabbing

a beefy finger at an intricately carved stone jaguar crouched among the plants.

Repressing a laugh, Randi explained, "It's a statue from Central America! Olga loves fantasy animals, and her husband is an art collector. There are ceramic and stone creatures throughout the garden."

"Garden! This place looks more like Tarzan's Retreat!" Benny wiped his jowled face with a handkerchief, missing the beads of sweat that ringed his receding hairline. "Where the hell is the Vasquez house, anyway?"

"Up ahead. This way." Randi walked on more slowly, making sure she didn't lose him again. "I'm taking you to the rear entrance. This is a shortcut. If we walked down the road from the parking area, the house would be a long block away."

"Probably would have been safer." Loosening the iridescent plaid tie, which matched his short-sleeved shirt, Benny glanced around suspiciously, as if every growing shadow held threat. "There aren't any snakes in here, are there?"

"No real ones," Randi said assuringly. "I thought you'd find walking through here adventurous."

"We've had enough adventure putting this damn science fiction miniseries together and getting the network to accept it. I know you're friends with Olga Griffin-Vasquez and all that, but you have to admit she hasn't been easy to work with. We have to meet at dusk because she's a *night person*. We have to meet at her house because it's *the dark of the moon*. And then we can't park in her driveway because it's her channel to *the outer world*. Strange woman!"

Randi listened to his complaints silently. She'd met with Benny many times in preparation for *Chrysalis*. Despite his paranoia, nervousness and constant complaining, she found the short, rotund man likable and sometimes humorous.

So far he'd not complained about Olga's demand that a woman—more specifically, Randi—direct the television miniseries based on her science fiction novel. Randi hoped no one knew she was Olga's godchild. She didn't need claims of nepotism added to the existing difficulties of being a woman director in the male-dominated film industry—an outspoken, individualistic one at that.

"If Olga weren't a best-selling science fiction author, the execs wouldn't have allowed her so much control," Benny went on. "This miniseries has got to pull in the ratings."

"Chrysalis will be a quality production. Why wouldn't people watch?"

"Oh, yeah. I know it'll be a smash hit. Don't mind me. I always worry. Gotta keep the network happy and my ulcers in business. I know we've got loads of talent involved with the project. Like yourself. I saw that commercial you directed where the motorcycle changes into a rocket ship and zooms into space. Great special effects!"

Glancing to her right, she saw the glimmer of red through the leaves. They were nearing Olga's oriental pagoda. How often Randi had come to her exotic playhouse to make wishes as a child. Well, now Olga had granted her the chance to achieve her dream—to direct a major dramatic production. Maybe the woman was her *fairy* godmother.

Pulling aside a palm frond as she stepped forward, Randi looked lovingly at the brightly painted structure. When she released the gigantic leaf, it made a resounding slap.

13

"Argh!"

Turning, she saw Benny struggling to remove the palm frond from his mouth. "Oh, I'm sorry! Did I hurt you?"

The producer won the battle with the greenery and stumbled toward her. He seemed breathless. "No. I'm okay. I lost my cigar, though. Hope nothing's flammable around here."

The cigar lay at the edge of the path. Randi picked up the smoking object with the tips of two fingers. Wrinkling her nose at its acrid smell, she held it out to him.

"Hope Tarzan doesn't mind cigars in his jungle and send Smokey the Ape after me or something." Benny quickly took the cigar and, without dusting it, stuck it back in his mouth. Looking around, he noticed the small building beneath the trees. "What's that?"

"It's a pagoda. An oriental temple."

"Oh. Someplace to pray to the jungle gods. Do you think they'd bless a miniseries?"

As they rounded the last bend in the path, they came face to face with Olga's three-story stone house. The structure rose in balconied terra-cotta tiers, decorated with lanterns, wind chimes and great hanging plants. Its many columns were Persian blue. Arabic latticework shielded most of the windows, and a circular iron staircase leading to the upper floors fronted two small towers. Reflected in the large, clear pool before it, the mansion seemed double in size.

"Shades of Cecil B. DeMille! What a set for a movie!" Benny's mouth gaped. "Olga must've built this place as an inspiration for her jungle planet in *Beyond Eden.*"

"It was built long before her last movie. This house and its grounds belonged to Olga's mother-in-law, Mae Ryan."

14

"The twenties movie star?" Benny peered at the foliage growing thickly on both sides of the pool. "How do you get to the place?"

"This way." Randi pointed to the steep, curving Chinese bridge.

"Oh. I thought it was just another decoration." Benny inched along after her. As they began to cross, he looked down into the pool's blue depths. "There are fish in there!"

"Of course. But, don't worry—no piranha."

"Any alligators?" At the top of the high arch, Benny stopped, puffing. "Whew!"

Randi took advantage of the pause to straighten her clothes. Rearranging the fedora on her head, she smoothed her chestnut hair back into its neat roll. Then she unfolded the tan linen jacket and eased it on over her rust-colored silk blouse.

"A little warm for a jacket, isn't it?"

"I feel more businesslike wearing one. I want to make sure this project starts off with a professional tone."

One would think that at the age of thirty-four, she wouldn't be so nervous. But because this was Randi's first assignment as director of a high-budget drama, she couldn't help it. Dressing the part couldn't hurt her confidence.

"Oh. I think we're headed in the right direction," Benny stated, continuing toward the house. "Got a good cast, for one thing. Jocelyn Morris looks perfect for the part of Lara."

"She looks like Lara, but can she act? Modeling for fashion magazines and doing a few sixty-second commercials isn't exactly the greatest preparation for a major acting role."

"I'm sure you'll be able to get the right stuff out of her."

Knowing he had confidence in her made her feel better. Randi cast him an appreciative sidelong glance.

"And Dion Hayden ought to inspire her," Benny went on. "He's had a lot of film experience. He's great box office and has a loyal following. Even if people don't like science fiction, they'll tune in to *Chrysalis* just to see *him.*"

"He's a showpiece, all right," Randi commented, starting up the circular staircase.

She couldn't quite eliminate the sarcasm from her tone. The popular star wasn't her choice as a leading man, but the network had wanted him and Olga had convinced her to acquiesce. In spite of her discomfort with the casting, Randi was determined to work smoothly with Dion.

"The guy's got charisma—a regular golden-boy image. Did you see him in his last movie?"

"No. I just didn't have the time. I was tied up with several projects, one right after the other, while that was out."

"Oh."

If the producer was curious, he didn't probe deeper. For that Randi was relieved. She didn't want to admit she'd carefully avoided every one of Dion's films. She just couldn't bring herself to go to one, even though as a responsible director, she should have made a point to see all of them.

They had reached the balcony of the second floor, where high french doors stood open. Pale golden light spilled out, and the murmur of voices trickled through to them.

"Looks like everyone's here!" Benny said, entering immediately.

Randi hesitated, drawing a deep breath. A thrill of trepidation ran through her. The sheer enormity of the project created enough pressure. Why did she have to deal with Dion, too?

As she entered the double-story drawing room, Randi eyed several crew members helping themselves to refreshments laid out on a long mirrored table. Looking beyond the spread of hors d'oeuvres, fresh pineapple, kiwi fruit, curried sauces and exotic breads, she saw Raoul Vasquez, Olga's distinguished-looking husband, dispensing drinks at the bar. She waved at Raoul and nodded to some of the others.

Randi scanned the crowd. She'd met with everyone of importance long before this assembly—everyone but Dion. The actor's involvement with a film shot in Europe had delayed the production of *Chrysalis* for several weeks. Unable to spot him, Randi wondered if he was still too busy to come to this very important meeting.

"Hi, Randi!" Supporting actress Nora Pratt had a delighted, childlike smile on her face. "Isn't this place too much? There's so much space!" The blonde twirled a few times, her arms spread wide. "I can *feel* it!"

"Watch your fruit!" Supporting actor Paul Tortorella took the plate from Nora's hand and shoved her down on a velvet couch. "Why don't you save your 'experiencing' for the filmed scenes?"

"She's practicing the Technique again," commented Jake Walker, Randi's young assistant director.

Jake had disdainfully explained Nora's involvement with the pop psychology acting method. Randi didn't

17

think it would hurt anything. Although her behavior might indicate otherwise, Nora was a skilled actress.

"Want some wine?" Jake asked.

"Sure."

While Jake got her drink, Randi automatically popped an hors d'oeuvre into her mouth, then realized she was standing too close to the refreshment table. She'd have to watch out. She didn't want to add extra calories to her carefully regulated diet.

The miniseries crew was seated in small groupings around the huge room. Jocelyn Morris had arranged her long, elegant body on an antique chaise and was checking her makeup in the huge gilt-framed mirror behind her. Several members of the technical crew were holding a conference near the onyx-manteled fireplace. Benny had made himself at home in an overstuffed chair, where he slurped a beer.

Where was Olga? And where was Dion? Randi wondered.

"This house is like an incredible movie set!" Nora exclaimed from her couch. "Look at the ceiling and the paintings up there—like Michelangelo! All this art surrounding us! Those weird winged creatures are a little spooky, though."

"They're griffins," Randi said as Jake handed her a glass of white wine. "Olga and Raoul have quite a miniature collection."

Nora continued. "I love all these mirrors reflecting everything back and forth. You know, you're looking at yourself looking at yourself. Wow, it's profound!"

"Uh huh." Paul quickly stuck a piece of pineapple in Nora's mouth while Jake aimed a disapproving scowl her way.

"Is Dion here?" Randi asked Jake.

"I saw him awhile ago."

"Well, I don't think we should hold up this meeting waiting for him."

"Good evening, darling." Olga Griffin-Vasquez set a glass bowl of mixed berries on the table and gave her godchild a hug without releasing Persephone, her favorite black cat. Stroking the animal's silky ears, Randi smiled into Olga's dark, kohl-lined eyes, then admired her ankle-length fringed silk shawl draped over a black dress and set off by her long silver hair.

"Don't you look dramatic! I've never seen that beautiful shawl before."

"Mae gave it to me as a wedding gift," Olga told her, referring to Raoul's mother. "It was part of her costume in *Blood and Sand*. I thought wearing a memento from the Valentino movie would bring good luck to our project."

"When's the meeting going to start, anyway?" asked Benny. "I'm ready."

"So am I," Olga agreed, adjusting the shawl over her tall, spare frame after setting the cat down.

Randi pulled up a high-backed Spanish chair, and the others turned their attention to the writer. Where was Dion? Did the ill-mannered actor think he could make his appearance whenever he felt like it, even if it meant everyone else had to wait for him? That had been his attitude when they worked on a feature film together three years ago, Randi the assistant director, Dion a rising star. Would the actor's current status as a film idol make him even more demanding and impossible? She shuddered when she thought about asking him to redo a scene again and again.

19

Randi put Dion out of her mind as Olga began the meeting.

"The reason I wanted to meet with all of you—"

But a scuffling noise muffled her words. All heads turned toward the source. As the drawing room's double-story central doors opened, their mirrored surfaces multiplied Dion Hayden's golden image; three Dions smiled at the crowd. His sensuous lips, high cheekbones and dark golden hair set over a perfect body combined for a blatant display of masculine beauty. He looked the part of the "golden god"—the title Hollywood had given him—his lines so perfect, he could be a statue.

All he needs is a pedestal, Randi thought with disgust.

"Sorry to keep you waiting," Dion said apologetically, his tone nonchalant. Running his eyes over his audience, he noisily pulled up a chair across from Randi and gazed at her intently.

Purposefully she turned her face away from him and back to Olga.

"I wanted to talk to you, the crew and actors of *Chrysalis,* personally before the shoot began." Olga's strong, unwavering voice drew the group's attention back to her. "This miniseries will be based on one of my best-selling books, as were the movies *Beyond Eden* and *Faster Than the Queen of Light.* Unlike those films, however, *Chrysalis* will be the first adaptation to be subject to my creative control as well as the producers'."

Randi felt Dion's blue eyes boring into her as Olga spoke, but she tried to avoid giving him the satisfaction of knowing she noticed. She'd have to maintain control over him or the shoot could turn into a disaster. She still remembered how Dion had almost made her lose her job the last time she'd worked with him. Because of an argument with the arrogant young actor, she'd missed an important meeting, causing her to make a costly scheduling mistake. He was bad news, there was no doubt about it.

"There will be no gratuitous battle scenes or fantastic weaponry added to this project," Olga continued. "I believe human experience can be an inner as well as an outer adventure, that our understanding of our own powers and emotions is more important than our invention of machinery."

Randi glanced toward Dion in spite of herself and found the young actor engrossed in Olga's speech. Maybe he'd learned to listen. Three years ago she'd prepped him for a fight scene in the western *Wrangler,* and he'd broken the jaw of another actor because he'd forgotten to pull his punch. More than once his childish tantrums had caused a lengthy shooting delay. He'd always been short on talent and long on ego. Could she hope for more now?

"These beliefs underlie the theme of *Chrysalis,* in which two contrasting cultures, one with developed psychic abilities and the other with incredible scientific technology, albeit useless on an unknown planet, are united through the love of a man and a woman." Olga paused, her black eyes flicking over the assemblage.

"I have the network's agreement on final say and have approved the script and casting. With everyone's cooperation, I think we can complete a successful production that will remain true to my book's original ideas. There is certainly enough talent in this room to make *Chrysalis* unique and outstanding!"

"I, for one, am looking forward to working on it!" exclaimed Dion. "I've read your book several times."

"And I've seen your performances several times." Olga smiled at him.

She sounded like a fan of Dion Hayden's! Randi still wondered why Olga had forced Dion on her, knowing how Randi felt. Her godmother couldn't have forgotten the confidences Randi had shared with her concerning the actor. When questioned, Olga had insisted that Dion was perfect for the part and, since Randi was a professional, she was sure her godchild could deal with the situation.

"Now I'll turn the rest of this meeting over to your very talented director, Randi St. Martin," Olga announced.

Starting slightly, Randi managed to say, "I'd like to take this opportunity to have each of the department heads tell you how his or her work is coming along. Why don't we start with costume design."

As the head designer reported to the gathering, Randi found her mind wandering and her eyes straying directly to Dion. His profile to her, his finely chiseled features formed a golden mask. Amazing how his smooth tan looked like it contained particles of the precious metal.

As if he knew she was studying him, Dion turned directly toward her. Startled, her eyes met his brilliant gaze, which enmeshed her in blue depths as alluring as Mediterranean waters. Dion's faultless lips split into a slow grin. Warmth spreading throughout her body, Randi quickly looked away.

And so it went. Those in charge of various phases of production reported on each department's progress as Randi introduced them one by one. She made suggestions several times but tried to keep the meeting moving. While Randi was able to keep track of the proceedings on one level, on another she grew more and more aware of Dion. She resented this unwanted intrusion into her thoughts.

As the director, she had to stay on top of everything that went on in this meeting.

"It sounds like the special effects are coming along well," Randi finally concluded. "If any of you would like to come to the studio to see the spaceship models before you go on location, you're certainly welcome to do so. Now that's it for business. Thank you all for coming. Olga?"

"Please feel free to stay for drinks," Olga said. "And if there's anything else I can do for you, let me know."

"How about a tour of this fabulous place?" Nora said enthusiastically. "That way we could all be more in touch with your personal reality, if you know what I mean."

Graciously Olga consented, suggesting they start with the grounds. The room quickly cleared, everyone following her and Raoul outside. Having been intimately acquainted with Olga's private domain since she was a child, Randi opted to finish her glass of wine on the balcony.

Looking out into the garden's lantern-lit depths, she reviewed the evening. Things had gone well in spite of her distraction. Feedback had been good, and she thought plans for the miniseries were shaping up. What a feeling of accomplishment she would have when the project was finished! Randi was determined it would be the foundation block of a great film career.

She listened to the gentle swish of leaves in the breeze and the sound of wind chimes. His step was so quiet, she barely heard him. Turning quickly to view the intruder, she was startled to see Dion.

"Why didn't you go on the tour?" she asked. It made her uneasy to be alone with him.

Dion lounged casually against a blue column. "I've

23

already seen everything. I took my own tour earlier. Besides," he said, leaning toward her, his voice intimate and silky, "I'd rather see you. It's been a long time, Ariadne."

At the use of her proper name, she drew back. "Not long enough."

"You're bitter," he stated.

"I don't hold anything against you."

"How about starting over, then? I've changed, you know."

Had he? What about the spectacular entrance he'd just engineered? But to be fair, Randi had to admit he'd faded into the background after the meeting started. Was it possible he was less egotistical than she remembered him as being? Not willing to admit it, she said, "I don't know what you mean."

"I've matured, learned a lot of things since I last worked with you."

"You needed to!"

"I want to show you I'm different."

As he moved closer, Dion's palm covered her hand on the railing, his fingers caressing her skin. Angrily she pulled her hand away.

"Then show me you're different professionally."

"And not personally? I've always remembered you and our night together as special."

"I'm sure you did!"

"You're angry because I didn't call you?"

"Still the same arrogant Dion Hayden." Randi shook her head. "I hate to disappoint you, but three years is a little long to wait by the phone. Especially after only one night together."

"I know it's been a long time and our time was brief,

but I thought about you a lot. When our eyes met tonight, I felt exactly like I did before."

"How convenient. Excuse me." Unwanted emotions kindling, Randi moved to the garden staircase and wound her way toward the ground. She had thought she was over Dion Hayden and the passionate night she'd allowed herself to spend with a pretty-faced actor who had been a young twenty-six to her mature thirty-one. The trouble was that in the ensuing three years she hadn't been able to forget the pleasure she'd felt making love to a man she'd professed to disrespect.

Randi had fought her attraction to Dion for the two months they'd worked together on that last project because she hadn't liked his unprofessional attitude. She'd been convinced he was in the business for fame and fortune and nothing else. Whenever he'd been asked to go beyond the basics in order to enhance the artistic quality of the production, he'd been uncooperative.

Even so, she'd found herself surrendering to Dion's charm on the night of the cast party celebrating the completion of the movie. Afterward she'd disrespected *herself*. What a fool she'd been! To make things worse, she'd been disappointed when he walked out of her life the next morning, never to contact her again.

"Randi?"

He'd followed her to the edge of the pool!

"What now?"

"I'm truly sorry about the past. I should have called, but I had good reasons. . . ."

"An apology isn't necessary. Forget it; I have."

"I can't forget you," he continued, catching her arms in his firm grasp. He was standing so close, his breath warmed her cheek with the light fragrance of wine. "I can't forget that night. It was poetry. I don't want to forget how your skin felt under my hands, or the texture of your hair."

With a deft gesture Dion removed her fedora and tossed it aside.

"What do you think you're doing?" she demanded.

His arm circled her waist securely, drawing her against him. "My foxy lady," he murmured, loosening her hair. "With your cleverness and charm, that russet in your eyes and hair."

He was doing it again, mesmerizing her with his soft, complimentary words! She wouldn't let him intrigue her, Randi decided. She opened her mouth to protest, but his was already descending. The softness of his lips made her forget words.

Gently but firmly he held her, her breasts pressed against his hard chest. As her body responded, her arms slipped around his trim waist. Unable to help herself, she traded him kiss for kiss, her tongue touching his in an erotic dance for two. She moved her hands higher, wanting to entwine her fingers in his springy curls.

He pulled away slightly. "We're poetry together. As sure as my name is Dionysus. We're like the lovers in the Greek myth."

The whispered words brought Randi back to her senses. Did he think she'd take him seriously, prattling on about melodramatic myths?

"How symbolic! I'm impressed. We're supposed to be lovers because of our names? Too bad I'm not in the mood for tall tales!"

She shoved herself away from him, pushing him slightly off balance.

Wavering back and forth, he cried, "Hey!"

Without thinking, Randi reached out to steady him and was caught in his arms. The next thing she knew, they were both falling toward the pool. "Oh, no!"

They hit the water together, splashes rising around them in a white spray. Suddenly freed, Randi went under, struggling with the water, hampered by her wet clothing. Finally she broke the surface. Treading, she spit out water and saw Dion swimming near her, a grin on his handsome face. So he thought this was fun, did he?

"You creep! Did you plan this little accident to rattle me?"

"What are you talking about?"

Incensed by the anger in his voice, Randi began swimming toward the pool edge.

"You're the one who pushed us into this pool," he said accusingly.

Before Randi could manage to haul herself out of the water, Olga led the touring group across the patio.

"Oh, look!" cried Nora. "They're practicing the pool scene. How experiential!" Immediately the actress sprinted to the water and jumped in.

The splash doused Randi as she clutched the pool edge.

"Come on in, Paul," called Nora to the supporting actor.

"Nora, this isn't a swimming party," Paul replied, disgust ripe in his voice as he steered his eyes toward Randi.

What must this group of professionals think about her? Randi started to pull herself out of the water, but a wiggling against her breasts made her freeze. "What the . . . ?" Quickly she ducked back down, loosening her blouse from the waistband of her slacks. When she

27

shook the garment, a four-inch fish swam frantically away from her.

"Ah, Randi, are you planning on playing around in there all night?" Jake asked with obvious disapproval. "I've got some scheduling I want to discuss with you before I leave."

"I'm coming right now, Jake."

Everyone seemed to stare at her as she lifted herself to sit on the tiled edge of the pool. Randi was thankful that the darkness hid the observers' expressions and that they, in turn, could not witness her flaming embarrassment. What a way to start the most important project in her directing career!

CHAPTER TWO

"All right, Jocelyn, let's rehearse your dialogue again," Randi told her, preventing the impatience she felt from creeping into her voice. If it took a dozen more run-throughs, they'd get this scene right!

"Wasn't I better this time?" the former model asked, turning her green eyes to her co-stars for confirmation.

They were all silent, even Nora, who usually had something positive to say about almost anything. Dion gave his leading lady an encouraging smile. Paul crossed his arms, rolled his eyes and aimed a heavy sigh of disgust at the nearby copse of white fir trees. The others stared at their toes.

Jocelyn seemed embarrassed, turning away and raking her fingers through her long dark hair.

Randi tried to put the aspiring actress at ease by giving her some insight to Lara's character. "You're in charge of the fuel-seeking expedition down to this uncharted planet; you have power but you don't abuse it. You're cool, levelheaded, extremely capable.

"When the villagers find you and the others, you realize their culture is equivalent to the Earth's Bronze Age. You doubt such 'primitives' can be of help in repairing the shuttle or communications or in finding a fuel supply for the mother ship. And you feel your technological culture makes you superior to the villagers. But you have to portray this without making the viewers dislike you. Control is the key. You're sure of yourself without being haughty."

"I think I understand her better now," Jocelyn said with a sigh.

"Then let's rehearse the scene again."

Jocelyn really did try, Randi told herself as she watched the fledgling actress. She needed a lot of work, however.

They'd shot all the studio scenes—the insides of both the mother ship and the exploration shuttle—before going on location to Sequoia National Park. As the competent, emotionally controlled technological expert, Jocelyn had been more than adequate with intensive rehearsals.

But what would happen when she had to change her character's personality as the script demanded? Did she have it in her to become the emotionally charged woman who opts to stay in the "primitive" world with Shann?

Randi didn't have time to hold Jocelyn's hand through the entire production. With the village still not completed, the miniseries was already behind schedule. Instead of filming the scenes she had planned for the first day of the location shoot—the entire village would have been required as a backdrop—Randi had to pick alternate scenes needing limited or no man-made sets.

At the moment her solace was that Dion had developed quite a bit of talent since they last worked together. Having matured from the cocky young man who got by on his looks into a competent actor, Dion didn't even mind doing multiple takes of a scene—another pleasant change. Perhaps some of his newfound expertise would rub off on Jocelyn.

"That sounded better, but let's try it again," Randi suggested when the actors finished the scene. "This time, Jocelyn, be more aware of your body," she told the tall, willowy woman. "Hold it tighter. You're in control, *always*. Don't think of it as a woman's body but as an efficient tool. That way, when your character softens later, the contrast will be more effective."

Randi rehearsed the actors again and again until it was time to break for lunch. They were only halfway through the day, and she was already exhausted. Jocelyn Morris was proving to be a director's challenge, to put it mildly.

"Time to refuel," Randi told them. "You have one hour."

Gathering her things, she didn't realize Dion was behind her until she heard his low-voiced approval.

"You've turned into quite a director."

"And your acting has improved considerably," Randi admitted, refusing to face the seductive golden glow that always seemed to surround him. Then Nora's enthusiastic prattle caught her attention.

"Listen, Jocelyn," Nora was saying. "You've got to learn to use the Technique more. You went through the basics in L.A., but it takes practice. Right now you're resisting. You've got to learn to attend and concentrate," she insisted, dramatically pressing the fingers of both hands to her forehead. "And you've got to sharpen your body sense."

"I guess I need more lessons," Jocelyn admitted.

"Too bad Kim Courtney can't tolerate the wilderness," Nora said, referring to the popular actress of the fifties who'd turned into a Hollywood cult figure and sought-after acting coach. "Otherwise she'd love to give us lessons right here on the set. Oh!" Nora squealed, jumping up and down. "Since Dion and I have been involved with her acting method for ages, we could help you! We could form a T-group of our own. Couldn't we, Dion?"

"Right. We can talk about it later," he suggested, moving to join them.

Then he turned around and aimed a broad wink at Randi before continuing to the lunch tables.

What was that supposed to mean?

"That Technique is a bunch of garbage. . . . Ah, sorry, boss lady," Paul Tortorella said.

Randi glanced at the actor who played the communications expert from the shuttle. His dark brown eyes were narrowed as he looked after the retreating figures. She knew Paul was a rebel in general with a reputation for having a hard time getting along with anyone.

"Why do you put down their acting method? If it works for them, what's the harm?"

"Aw, come on. The whole idea of the Technique is to live the part you're playing, on and off the set. You're supposed to integrate the reality of your character into your everyday life. You tell me how Jocelyn is supposed to pretend she's this technological whiz when Miss Cover Girl probably doesn't have half a brain in her head."

"I'm sure she'll do fine, Paul. Just worry about your own lines." Randi coolly turned and headed for the lunch line herself.

Paul's attitude wasn't going to help make things pleasant on the set, Randi thought, then soothed herself by absorbing the view.

On location in a wilderness area of the Sierra Nevada Mountains, they were camped in a comfortably warm, lush pine forest that would be home base for the next six weeks. Patches of ponderosa and sugar pine joined the white firs. Small meadows graced the slopes around them.

That the Sierras provided such contrasting scenery always amazed Randi. She turned and looked down on the village being built just below in the steep foothills. The area was distinguished by rolling grassy meadows, clusters of live oaks, sycamores and low-growing chaparral. In spring it had been carpeted with wild-flowers of every hue, but now, at the height of summer, the landscape was dry and almost forbidding by contrast.

"What can I get for you, Ms. St. Martin?" one of the caterers asked.

Tantalized by the smell of food cooked in the open, Randi was hard pressed not to give in and ask for a little of everything. She had to keep strict control over herself or she'd gain back the five pounds she'd recently lost and never lose the other five she hoped to get rid of on this shoot. Weight control was an ongoing battle, but one she was valiantly determined to win.

"Black coffee and a piece of that pineapple will be fine."

"No it won't," a familiar voice stated from behind. Randi found herself being pulled away from the table. "I've already seen to Ms. St. Martin's lunch," Dion assured the caterer.

"What do you think you're doing?"

"Preventing you from starving yourself. You've lost weight." It sounded like a criticism. "You could use a good meal."

"B-but . . . !" Randi sputtered.

"No ifs, ands or buts! You need to keep up your

strength if you plan to get through this afternoon. You're having lunch with me!"

Resigning herself to doing so or spending the rest of her free hour arguing, Randi allowed Dion to lead her away from the tables filled with chattering cast and crew. His destination was a quiet spot under the trees, where he'd spread a blanket and left two plates brimming with food.

"I can't eat that much!"

"You can do anything you set your mind to. It was one of the things I always admired about you."

"Admired? You could have fooled me!" Randi said, resenting his reference to the past.

"So I was immature and liked to argue."

"And you don't now? As I recall, you didn't think I did much of anything right three years ago."

"Oh, yes I did."

The very personal note in his tone got to Randi. His Mediterranean blue eyes sparkled with mischief. Images of that one night they had spent together flooded her mind.

"I'm talking about professionally!"

"Of course. What did you think I meant?" he asked, all innocent affrontery. "Now eat."

Flustered, Randi focused on her plate. Grilled chicken, brown rice, corn on the cob, spinach salad, fresh fruit with walnut and pecan chunks, and a thick slice of whole grain bread stared back.

"This is enough food for three days," she muttered. "Or for three people!"

"Everything there is good for you. Eat."

Reluctantly she did as Dion bade, all the while trying to concentrate on the nutritious food before her. It

34

proved to be an impossible task. While the succulent chicken, tangy fruit and tasty bread slipped into her mouth, her traitorous eyes and thoughts wandered off into forbidden territory. For once she forgot to count calories.

Dion Hayden was still a magnificent male, Randi admitted to herself, even more so now that a few years had added an appealing maturity to his perfect features and a muscular breadth to his faultless body.

The most enticing thing about him, however, was his curly hair, the natural golden locks grown almost to shoulder length for his role as Shann. In their shaded retreat under a huge pine, Randi knew his hair glowed with a vibrancy all its own. Her fingers itched to test their texture, to discover whether the curls were soft and silky yet delightfully springy, as she remembered.

"Like what you see, Foxy?"

Realizing he'd caught her staring—and most probably read her thoughts—Randi almost choked on her food. Luckily her throat cleared at the first cough.

"Don't call me that ridiculous name!"

"I remember a night you didn't think it ridiculous," he said and sighed, setting down his plate. "And you really are a very foxy lady, you know."

"Dion!"

"Say my name again," he coaxed as though she hadn't shrilled it. He was grinning at her, a hint of straight white teeth peeking from behind his sculpted lips. "Your voice is music to my ears."

He was doing it to her again! In spite of her resolve to avoid being sucked in by his charm, Randi felt herself spiraling toward that disastrous state. There was that stupid answering grin plastered to her own lips, and she

35

didn't object when he took the empty plate from her nerveless hands and set it on top of his own.

"Dion," she whispered, shaking her head in exasperation.

"That's better."

Then he took one of her hands and brought it to his lips, kissed the palm and moved it to the side of his head. Automatically her fingers tangled in the locks there, and she discovered they were indeed soft, silky and springy, just as she had remembered.

Moving pictures stored in her memory like film clips in an archive were projected to haunt Randi as she stared into his eyes: Dion's beautiful body naked under hers; Dion's gentle hands touching her breasts with reverence; Dion's face filled with passion as he cried out her name, shuddering with the ultimate pleasure.

Her body responded to the vivid imagery, the feel of his head under her fingertips and his masculine scent that suddenly seemed overpowering. Without his so much as touching her, Randi's breasts seemed to swell and her nipples to tighten. A warmth began to pulsate from her center until every nerve in her body tingled, and her heart thudded wildly until the blood sizzled through her veins.

"Don't ever hesitate to tell me what you want," he said softly, inching his head toward hers. "I always take orders from my director."

The teasing words were like a splash of ice water on her overheated brain. What in the world was she thinking of? Randi pressed her hand against Dion's chest to stop his lips from touching her own.

"Then as your director, I'm ordering you to leave me alone!"

Randi was up and moving away from their sheltering pine tree within seconds.

"Almost always," she heard him call after her. The words were followed by a deep-throated chuckle that raised the hairs on the back of her neck.

"Troublemaker!" Striding toward the eating area, Randi mumbled to herself until she noticed Jake Walker standing several yards away, his hands planted on his hips. Had he been watching her? How much had he seen? Plenty, if the expression on his rugged face was any indication.

"Yes, Jake?" she asked curtly.

"I thought I ought to remind you lunch hour's almost up. Jocelyn was wanting to talk to you before you started this afternoon's rehearsal."

"Oh. Well, thank you."

"I also thought you'd like to know Chuck's ready to start shooting as early as you can get the cast together in the morning," Jake said, walking alongside Randi. "He's checked the shots you wanted and says they'll work without the village being completed."

"Fine. Why don't you arrange breakfast for sunrise, then alert makeup and wardrobe?"

Jake went off to do as she asked. While she was looking for Jocelyn, Randi berated herself. What a fool! After Olga's party, she had vowed to treat Dion Hayden in a businesslike manner. There would be nothing personal between them, she'd decided. And the very first time he got her alone with him, look what had happened.

In the intervening weeks Randi had convinced herself Dion wasn't really interested in her. He'd been testing her on the night of the party, nothing more. That must have been his plan, since he never had called her after the party. What did she expect? He hadn't called her in three years!

"There you are," Jocelyn said as Randi approached. "Do you have a few minutes to discuss something with me?"

Randi put aside her angry thoughts of him while Jocelyn poured out all her doubts about her own performance.

"Hold on a couple of minutes" came a loud voice from the other side of the fifteen-foot gates. "We gotta fix Shirley's makeup again."

"That Shirley certainly is being resistant, isn't she?" Nora commented to the other actors.

"I don't believe it. Now she's trying to apply her crazy acting psychology to a goat!" Paul blared in disgust.

"Who are you calling crazy?"

"Please!" Randi pleaded. "I know you're getting tired of waiting and it's very hot out here in the sun, so why don't we all go sit in the shade somewhere and take it easy for a few minutes."

"Yeah, okay, boss lady, but I'm not going to sit with the method actress here," Paul replied as he went off to find his own shade. "Some of that garbage might rub off on me!"

"He's so mean!"

"Listen, Nora. Paul's insecure, but he shouldn't take it out on someone else," Jocelyn told her, pulling the blonde under the shade of the nearest oak tree. "Try not to let him bother you. You're a terrific actress."

Another problem! That was all she needed—fighting between two actors who were supposed to be lovers by the end of the miniseries.

At least the first scene they shot that morning—the villagers finding the stranded explorers—had gone well. But now they couldn't seem to get started on the next. Every time Randi thought they were all set, Shirley—made up to represent an alien animal—managed to remove the fake flat horn that curved around her eyes like a half-mask, or to pull off some of the added shaggy fur attached to her chest and underbelly.

Spotting her assistant director with Sally Brown, the woman in charge of script continuity, Randi waved them over to her.

"Jake, what's going on?"

"Shirley's got a thing for lover boy, not unlike some human females. Every time she gets near Dion, she rubs against him and screws up her makeup job."

Sure that he was comparing the goat's reaction to her own of the previous day, Randi was furious. Determined that Jake wouldn't have the satisfaction of knowing his rude remark had disturbed her—especially not in front of Sally, with whom she'd never before worked—she was determined to speak calmly.

"Can't we switch goats?"

"Only if you want to take out the bit where she pulls the analyzer out of Jocelyn's hand. Shirley's the only goat trained to do it."

"All right. We'll try again. Let me know when she's ready."

Jake jogged off, but Sally remained behind. Quietly she jotted notes on the script attached to her clipboard. Randi was relieved the other woman didn't seem to suspect that Jake's comment had a personal meaning.

So the goat had a thing for Dion! Randi thought, looking toward the wooden walls and gates. Although the actor hadn't done anything wrong, he was still the source of the problem. In a strange, roundabout way, Dion was causing difficulty on the set all over again.

"Oh, Ms. St. Martin," Sally said, looking up. "It's going to be a pleasure working with you." A glimmer of a smile played around her lips, and her intent brown eyes met Randi's directly. "It's difficult being a woman in this business. If you ever need someone to talk to, I've been told I'm a good listener."

So she must have understood Jake's comment after all. "Thank you, Sally—"

"Randi," Jake called from the gates, interrupting her. "We're ready to roll."

Randi eyed the crew. Both camera units were ready, the operators standing by for orders. The sound man gave her the high sign.

"Places."

Paul and Nora as Reed and Mallory were to band together in this scene. Could they do it without arguing? Randi wondered. They'd better! They were both professionals. Since this scene would introduce Dion as Shann, Randi hoped he'd be just as professional and not give her any trouble. Would Jocelyn remember all the insight about Lara's character? The actress's knuckles were white as she gripped her prop life analyzer.

Once all the talent was in place, Randi crossed her fingers. Now if only Shirley would leave well enough alone!

"Cameras . . . and action!"

Several "primitives" dressed in leather or woven medieval-type costumes led the "off-worlders" in their quilted futuristic garb toward giant wooden walls rising up the side of a hill. The natives spoke in a mutated version of

40

English. One of the women touched a blue stone set in an unusual copper necklace and softly chanted with her eyes half-closed.

"Shann . . . Shann . . . Shann!"

"I can't quite make out what they're talking about," Lara said. "This Shann must be a person of importance."

"Maybe Shann is one of their gods," Reed suggested.

"More likely their leader," Mallory insisted.

The small group stopped outside the walls. A loud creak indicated they had been spotted, and the four people from the downed space shuttle tensed. Mallory gripped Reed's arm.

Suddenly Shann was revealed, his golden image intensified by the bright sun and reflected in the bronze decorations on the inside of the fifteen-foot gates. Dressed in an open leather tunic, breechcloth and leggings, he seemed to revel in the startled expressions of the offworlders.

Randi blinked. This scene was certainly familiar. Hadn't Dion made a similarly grand entrance at Olga's party?

"Are you the one called Shann?" Lara asked boldly.

Shann strode to the group, followed by an eager Shirley, who unsuccessfully tried to butt him in the rear.

"I am. Welcome to Chrysalis."

"You speak our language?"

Shann nodded. "As do several others in the clan Yahanschil."

"Then perhaps you can help us," Lara said, waving her life analyzer as she spoke. "We need to find fuel for our mother ship."

At this point Shirley was supposed to approach the woman and take the prop from her hand. Her handler

41

stood to the side and gave her the signal. Randi silently urged the goat on, but the animal was interested only in the magnificent man next to her. Shirley rubbed her nose on one of Dion's leggings, then, grabbing the material with her teeth, she ripped it off!

A titter began through the crowd, quickly spreading into an uproar.

"Cut!" Randi yelled at the top of her voice.

Unbelievable! Trouble did seem to follow Dion. Although he hadn't exactly created the problem, he was still the source.

As the laughter died, Randi heard Dion say with a chuckle, "Well, she's not the only female who's ever wanted to take off my pants."

Startled, Randi turned. Dion was staring directly at her!

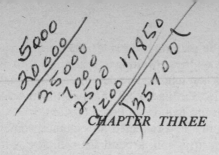

CHAPTER THREE

"Beautiful scenery out here," Benny Fields said, as if he could see it by the soft glow of the kerosene lanterns. "Nice mountains and everything."

"Uh-huh."

Sitting across from the producer at one of the wooden tables in the commissary area, Randi watched the smoke from his ever-present cigar drift upward before disintegrating into the darkness. If only her troubles with the miniseries would disappear as easily, she thought, sipping her strong black coffee. Since Benny's arrival with the supply truck, she'd been trying to give him a positive progress report between his rambling comments.

"This place makes a perfect setting for the story, right?"

"It couldn't be better. Unless you want to transport us to the Himalayas or the Andes."

"Too expensive!"

"Benny, I was only kidding."

"Well, maybe the Andes would have been better, but we have to make do with the resources we have. Settings . . . actors . . ."

"Sure."

Randi was growing tired of listening to Benny's small

43

talk. When was he planning to leave? The supply truck was unloaded, the driver waiting for him. And Randi wanted to go to her tent and review the coming day's shooting schedule. She had a lot of work to do before retiring for her usual five or six hours of sleep.

The cast and crew had retreated after dinner, some to their tents, others to a spot around the campfire, while she and Benny had lingered over a cup of coffee. A few yards away, however, Dion had made himself a comfortable reading nook from a couple of benches. His golden head shone under the soft lantern light. Randi gave the actor a curious sidelong glance when she noticed his book —a text on parapsychology.

"You have to adapt your raw materials," Benny went on. "Just like you have to adapt your own expectations to what the network executives want."

The producer now had Randi's complete attention. She didn't like the sound of that.

"I mean, have you ever thought about how a simple change—like a new title, for instance—might appeal to a broader viewing audience? *Chrysalis* isn't exactly a household word."

"Perhaps not, but it fits the theme of the production."

"Yeah, but what's so important about that? Another title might be better. Give it more pizzazz. How about *Invasion of the Earth Women?*"

The suggestion was so absurd Randi had to chuckle. "Sounds like a B movie from the fifties. Why don't we call it *Attack of the Giant Artichokes?*"

Suspiciously Benny said, "I don't remember any artichokes in this film."

"And there aren't enough females on the spaceship to call it *Invasion of the Earth Women,* either."

"Uh . . . couldn't we add more?" Randi's smile died when she noted Benny's serious expression. "We could put them in skimpy costumes," he went on. "Oh, something like silver bikinis with thigh-high boots. It would add visual interest for the viewers, since this isn't an action-oriented miniseries. No heavy battle scenes or anything."

Randi hoped he was joking. Her tone light, she suggested, "Why don't we do something different? Let the men wear the skimpy outfits. That should appeal to the women viewers. We could dress Dion in a gold lamé loincloth."

Hearing a loud snort, Randi glanced at Dion long enough to appreciate his charming grin before it disappeared behind the book, then she turned her attention back to the producer. Clearly uncomfortable, Benny was puffing so rapidly on his cigar that smoke billowed around them. Randi drank her coffee to calm herself and refilled the cup.

"All right, Benny. What's going on?" she finally asked, breaking the uncomfortable silence. "You're not tossing out these ideas just for fun, are you?"

"The uh . . . big boys at the network . . ." Benny paused and cleared his throat. "Uh . . . they wanted me to approach you with a few suggestions for changes."

A chill knotted Randi's stomach, and she tried to soothe it with more hot coffee before demanding, "Why? Why on earth would the network want to turn a serious project into a farce?"

"Now, wait a minute. Don't get mad. The execs are only trying to protect their investment. You know, make up for some of the weak points in the production." Benny

45

shook his cigar at her. "You know as well as I do that Jocelyn Morris isn't A-one acting material."

"Hiring a beautiful model rather than an accredited actress was the network's choice, not mine. You know why I agreed to use her. It was one of the conditions the 'big boys' insisted on in exchange for creative control." She should have known they would be eager to renege on their promises, Randi thought, absently rubbing her suddenly upset stomach. And they'd use any excuse to do so, even reasons based on gossip, which was always rampant on any set. "Besides which, I've been coaching Jocelyn and she's been working very hard. She's doing just fine!"

"Uh, that's not what they've heard. And what about the two supporting actors? They hate each other. And you're running behind schedule. That makes the money men very nervous."

"Now that the village is finished, I'll be able to get the production back on schedule by the end of the week," Randi assured him. "As for Paul and Nora, they're professionals. Any personality conflicts will not be reflected in their performances. Where are the network executives getting all this information, anyway?"

"Not from me!"

Randi glowered around the area, as if she could immediately find a culprit. She noted Dion's questioning stare. Sure he had heard everything, she was embarrassed. Of all the people who could have witnessed this humiliating scene, why did it have to be him?

Doubly irritated, she snapped, "I'd love to know who's telling tales around here. More important, I want to know why the network has decided to get involved at this stage of the game. Every production has some rough spots, especially at the beginning of the shoot."

"Uh . . . from what I understand, the execs want to keep close tabs on this production because you're . . . uh . . . new."

"Aha. So now we're getting down to the real problem. They think I can't handle my job!"

"No, that's not it. But they strongly suggest you consider reducing the serious nature of *Chrysalis*. Give it a broader appeal. Be more in touch with the limits of your material."

"And with my own limitations as director?"

"Hey, don't take it personally. They just want a few changes."

"How else am I supposed to take it? They can take their changes and . . ." Randi didn't finish telling Benny what the executives could do with their changes. What if he agreed with them? Instead she asked, "What about you, Benny? What do you think I should do?"

The producer examined his cigar before answering. "I'm not going to tell you what to do. You'll be fine doing it your own way. But maybe you should think about the options before you decide. Consider your future. More jobs with the network. Recommendations. You might need some friends in high places someday."

"I prefer friends who respect me."

"Is that what you want me to tell them?"

"No. Tell them . . ." A wry smile twisted Randi's lips as an inspiration hit her. "Tell them to talk to Olga. If they can get her to agree to any of their changes, I'll be more than happy to carry them out," she said, knowing the author would have a fit if approached with such ridiculousness. "Otherwise things stay as they are."

Rising from the table, Benny sighed. "Okay. Have it your way. I hope everything goes well. Hey Steve, you

47

got the dailies?" he shouted to the driver, referring to the exposed film that would be brought back to Los Angeles for processing.

"Yeah. In the truck."

Sticking his cigar back into his mouth, Benny ambled forward, pausing for a short coughing fit. "Whew! I'd better get back to the city fast! This fresh air is killing me!"

Randi waved to the producer as he climbed the high step of the truck with difficulty, his cigar jammed between his gritted teeth.

"See you in a few days," she called after the departing vehicle.

Although she tried to be optimistic about the indirect confrontation with the network by telling herself she'd won this round, Randi was worried. Who was feeding negative information to the outside? If they had been on a sound stage in L.A., she could blame the rumor mill, but out here on location there had to be a spy in her midst, someone hired by the network to report details of every little problem so they'd have an excuse to take away her creative control. But who was the traitor?

Thinking about it, Randi came to an uneasy conclusion. Not wanting to believe her assistant director would betray her, she had to admit Jake Walker was the most logical suspect. The muscles in her neck and back felt like they'd tightened into knots, and she rolled her shoulders to loosen them. Was she going to have to start watching Jake in return? she wondered uneasily.

About to take another swallow of coffee, Randi stared at the mug, then put it roughly on the table.

"What's the problem?" Dion asked, closing his book

48

and watching her closely. "Benny? The network? The world in general?"

"None of the above," Randi responded shakily. She'd forgotten Dion was nearby. "It's just that this wretched coffee is upsetting my stomach."

It really was. Not only was her stomach upset, it felt like it was on fire.

"I'll make you some herbal tea." Before she could protest, Dion was out of his seat and at one of the portable gas stoves. He placed a kettle already filled with water on a burner, then started a flame. "It'll do wonders for your stomach."

"I'm not so sure. When it feels this bad, nothing seems to help."

"Ulcers, huh?"

"That's all I need!"

"Haven't you asked a doctor about it?"

"I don't have time to go to a doctor."

"You know, you should take a break once in a while. Stop to smell the forest . . ."

"In other words, all work and no play makes Jill a dull girl," Randi said sarcastically. "Thanks for the advice, but I take my work seriously."

"So do I," Dion insisted.

Randi thought that now it appeared he did. She hoped his attitude would last.

Handing her a cup of tea, Dion wedged a lean hip onto the edge of the table. "All I was trying to say is that a little relaxation wouldn't hurt you. That and the proper nourishment plus a little exercise will keep you fit."

His voice was gentle and coaxing, making it hard for her to be angry with him even though she resented anyone telling her what to do. Aware of his muscular thigh on the table only inches from her hands, Randi forced herself to grip the mug. She felt like telling him she didn't need his advice or his concern. She could take care of herself.

Instead, she drank the tea.

"Like it?"

"M-m-m."

They sat in companionable silence, and Randi was amazed at how good—and how natural—being near him felt. Three years ago she and Dion couldn't have spent two minutes together without getting into an argument. Perhaps he really had changed, in more ways than one. Even realizing that, she was startled at his next words.

"I admire you, Randi St. Martin."

"Why? Because I dare to drink your tea?"

He laughed softly, and the sound affected her more than she liked. It made her uneasy. It made her remember.

"No. Because you wouldn't buckle under pressure from the big boys. You're honest and you've got the courage to carry out your convictions. You do what you think is right. I've always admired those traits in you. I was even jealous of them once upon a time."

"You were jealous of me? Come now. You have everything anyone in this business could want—looks, charm . . . a great profile," she added lightly, noting how the warm lantern light rimmed his golden hair and set it ablaze.

"Talent?"

She ignored his amused expression as well as his casually issued question. "Everything came so easy for you." Career advancement had always been a struggle for her, she thought resentfully.

"Yes. Far too easy," he said quickly, before changing the subject. "How's your stomach?"

"Surprisingly enough, better." She hadn't realized it until he'd asked, but the burning sensation had died down. "Thanks. Now if only your magic potion could soothe the knots in my neck as well."

"Tension really got to you. Tell Dr. Dion where it hurts."

"So he can make that all better too?" Randi chuckled, yet she felt a little thrill shoot through her still-tender stomach. "I hate to disappoint you, but I stopped playing doctor when I was five years old."

"But I've got new rules. Care to try my version?"

Oh, she was tempted!

"I've got to get back to my home-away-from-home to do some work," Randi told him, neatly avoiding his question.

"I'll walk you there."

No was on the tip of her tongue, yet the word didn't slide off nearly as easily as he did from his perch on the edge of the table. Before she knew it, Randi found herself being escorted to her tent, which had been erected a hundred yards or so from the others. She'd wanted to ensure her privacy and a quiet place to work at night. Now it loomed ahead, a dark shape amid a dozen pine trees, faintly outlined by the beam of his flashlight—a haven for her imagination.

Dion didn't touch her but quietly walked alongside, his shoulder scant inches away. Even so, Randi fancied that the comforting heat of his flesh warmed her own. She hugged herself, trapping her hands under her armpits so they wouldn't be tempted to reach out and touch the beautiful male body she couldn't forget.

51

The strange sensation that spiraled through her was compounded by the absence of sound as they walked. Their footsteps were muffled by several inches of pine needles covering the forest floor. Dion moved beside her in silence. What was he thinking? Was he remembering how well their bodies had matched and mated one glorious summer eve? Did he remember her abandoned response to him?

Randi felt herself blushing at the memory and imagined that Dion could see the color staining her face even though darkness surrounded them. As they approached her tent, she forced herself to pierce the peaceful stillness.

"I left my lantern hanging from that tree. Would you aim the flashlight over there so I can get it?"

"Sure."

Ignoring the protesting stiffness in her shoulders and neck, Randi reached up to untie the knot in the line from which her lantern hung. Either her fingers fumbled or the knot refused to give, but somehow, in her determination to undo it, she strained the tight muscles.

"A-ah!"

"What's wrong?"

Randi didn't answer as she gripped the back of her neck with both hands. With her eyes squeezed shut, she willed the pain to go away. As she moaned, she heard Dion sigh.

"You should have let me help."

He was next to her then, his gentle hands removing hers. He covered the sore area with his warm palms, using only slight pressure to make the muscles relax.

Randi lowered her arms and sighed. "I guess you're right. Dr. Dion is very good with his hands."

There was a tinge of amusement in his voice when he answered, "I'm glad you finally realized it."

I *remember,* she thought.

"I'll get the lantern."

Removing it easily, he set the lantern on the ground to light it. Then he unzipped the doorway of her tent and held the screen open for her.

"Come on," he said. "The doctor's not through."

Randi hesitated, knowing she shouldn't even think of letting him into her tent. "What if someone sees us?" Although that was one consideration, Randi's real fear was what could happen if they were alone.

"Come on. What good will you be if you can't move tomorrow?"

The soft words were seductive, and Dion did make a lot of sense. Awkwardly Randi stooped to enter her own tent, then stood in the middle of the small space, aware of her accelerated heartbeat.

"Take off your jacket and lie down."

Randi did as instructed while he zipped the screen closed behind him. She stripped off her cotton jacket and threw it over a piece of luggage, then she sat cross-legged on the air mattress. Hanging the lantern from a hook in the center of the tent, Dion looked around, his blue eyes flicking from her to the pile of scripts and notes strewn on the floor next to her.

"Do you have any kind of lotion?"

"There."

Randi pointed to a soft bag filled with cosmetics and soaps, then studied him as Dion searched it and found the bottle of moisturizer. Her heart seemed to skip a beat as his eyes met and locked with hers when he loomed above her. Shoving the mass of papers on the floor out of his way, he lowered himself to the mattress.

"I can't do a thorough job if you insist on sitting."

After loosening the tank top from the waistband of her pants, Randi stretched out on her stomach, her upper body resting on a pillow. Hearing him stir, she pressed her forehead into the pillow and closed her eyes.

Every nerve in her body responded when Dion positioned himself over her, his jean-clad knees straddling her waist, his firm buttocks lightly resting on her own. Randi's thin cotton clothing hardly protected her from the delicious sensation of his warmth. Her flesh tingled.

Why was she allowing this? Randi demanded of herself when she tensed at the tightening of her nipples. She was thankful her breasts were pressed into the air mattress so Dion wouldn't know how much he affected her.

"Try to relax, will you, or this will be an exercise in futility."

"I am relaxed!" she insisted.

"Like hell you are!" he growled.

So much for trying to hide her involuntary reactions from Dion. But then hadn't he always been aware of how much he affected her? The difference was that three years ago he would have stimulated her very personal response to feed his own ego. Instinct told Randi that now, while Dion might enjoy her reaction to him, his first concern was her welfare.

A soft squish preceded the delightful sensation of cool liquid on her neck, and a light scent of almonds wafted to her. Randi tried not to squirm. She concentrated on other things—the shoot the next day, the big scenes with dozens of extras the following week, the special effects being created back in L.A.—but through it all she was aware of his hands on her flesh.

He smoothed the moisturizer on her neck, along her shoulders and over the top of her back. His palms covered and warmed her muscles, sending a spreading heat throughout the rest of her body. Then his fingers pushed and probed, finding the knots of tension and working them out. In spite of herself, in spite of her awareness of him not as an actor working for her but as a man she had once made love to and still desired, she relaxed.

It was more of a languor, actually, that stole over Randi without her being aware of exactly when it happened. She didn't want to fight it but gave in to the bone-melting sensation. No protest passed her lips when Dion's hands reached under the tank top and smoothed the flesh along both sides of her spine, then spread outward to the fullness of her breasts.

Randi sucked in her breath and heard a like sound above her.

"Foxy?"

She twisted her upper body toward him, then realized Dion was moving with her and helping her turn around fully. On her back, Randi gazed up at the man who was still over her, one hand under her tank top, curving around the side of her breast. She reached up to lace her fingers in the golden curls haloed by the soft light of the lantern.

It seemed to be the encouragement he awaited.

Dion lowered his head so slowly Randi knew he was giving her time to move away if she would. Instead she sped the embrace by tugging at his curls.

Their mouths met in a glorious reunion, one Randi knew she'd craved since the night at Olga's. How wonderfully familiar his lips felt slanted over hers! Could she really remember their taste and texture so well after all this time?

After kissing her until she was breathless, Dion teased Randi by pulling away slightly so he could run his mouth around the edges of her lips until she was ready to scream in frustration. When her teeth trapped his lower lip in a demanding nip, he gasped, and the expelled air tickled her nose.

Randi giggled.

"So, you think my kisses are funny, do you, foxy lady? I'll teach you not to laugh at an enamored man!"

"But . . . !" was all she had time to sputter before his mouth covered hers once more.

This time his kiss had lost its playfulness, and in response, so did Randi. Dion plundered her with his mouth. At the first touch of his tongue, she was filled with a blazing sensation that only his hands and his body could quench. Randi slid against him, pressing her breast into his waiting palm.

His fingers moved slowly, spreading wide and fanning the delicate flesh. Dion rubbed her nipple with his thumb, the light strokes irritating the sensitive peak so that her passion centered there. Then his mouth left hers to find her other breast hidden under the tank top. He nipped and teased it through the material until she throbbed with an almost painful desire.

Randi moaned and slipped down, moving her breast away from his mouth. Moving her hips securely into position with his, she wedged against the hardness she sought. His immediate physical response gratified Randi.

"Oh, Foxy," Dion breathed into her ear. "Do you have any idea what you're doing to me?"

She kissed his throat in response.

Pressing himself against her, Dion groaned. Randi thought it the most beautiful sound she'd ever heard. She pressed back but was startled when he pulled away.

"Dion?" she whispered.

After a final quick kiss on her lips, he pulled out of her reach, kneeling at the edge of the air mattress. His chest heaving, Dion ran a shaky hand through his hair. His blue eyes bore into her, making Randi flush. He wanted her as much as she did him. Then why was he leaving? Dion had always had the power to confuse her.

He was already up and moving to the opening of the tent when his lips curved into a grin. "Good things are worth waiting for. Dream of me, foxy lady."

What good things did he mean? Her? Or him? Was Dion's ego hard at work once more? Convincing herself that he meant their coming together, Randi was mollified if slightly frustrated.

No doubt she would dream of Dion, just as he'd ordered. Hadn't she been doing so for the past week? Strangely enough, they were beginning to shoot the dream sequences in which Shann projected his image into Lara's mind. Did Dion have the same power over her? Randi mused.

Disgusted with herself, Randi flopped back onto her stomach. Why did she have such a difficult time understanding Dion and his motivations? Or herself and how easily she responded to him, for that matter? She was a skilled film director surviving in a highly technical sphere, yet she didn't understand the powerful inner emotions Dion evoked in her.

Even when they'd worked together before, Randi had been torn between disrespecting Dion as an actor and appreciating him as a human being and as a man. His spontaneity had always infected her. Randi had to admit that his tantrums had been offset to some extent by his natural warmth. From the first time she met him, Randi had been drawn to Dion as if by some unknown power.

Randi yawned, too tired to delve further into the illogical realm of romantic attraction. She eyed the scripts and notes shoved into a pile on the floor but decided she'd rather rise early than attack them in her current frame of mind.

At least she'd gotten one thing out of their frustrating tryst: She could understand how Lara felt.

CHAPTER FOUR

"I hate this planet!" cried Nora. "These inhabitants have strange powers and are trying to take over my mind!" Then, casting a fearful glance over one shoulder, the actress scurried away.

Not sure whether she had heard Nora correctly, Randi stopped dead in her tracks, once again assuring herself she was witnessing Nora practicing a Technique exercise, total character immersion, rather than a filmed scene. Randi hadn't expected to meet the actress while checking out the location for a crowd sequence. What was she going to do with Nora? Why did the actress have to go so far? Her "living" of the character was a little out of hand.

Randi shook her head and moved along the hillside, which was dappled with the narrow shadows of towering fir trees. Nora's behavior was definitely getting on her nerves.

For the past week the usually bubbly blonde had been wandering around camp "in character," acting out the paranoia of a logical scientist faced with an illogical psychic world. Once Randi had found Nora hiding behind a tent and muttering to herself. It was one thing to immerse herself in her character on the set, if only the young woman would act normally when she wasn't in the

59

process of doing a scene before a camera! Nora was doing a great job as her miniseries character, but Randi missed the presence of the real off-camera person, with all her warmth and frivolity.

Skirting some partially submerged boulders nestled against the steep hillside in slanted slabs, Randi noted the smattering of white paint that looked like natural markings on a massive rock. The extras would be led this way by Dion, past the boulders and down through an area thought clear enough for easy passage. The crowd's escape from an off-worlder holding a laser gun would be filmed from different angles by three camera units.

"Look good?" asked cinematographer Chuck Brockman as Randi stepped over the cables lying around the camera equipment.

She nodded. "We're almost ready to roll."

Chuck moved behind the master camera while Randi signaled Jake and the people milling around in the clearing near a growth of yellow pines. The assistant director relayed her instructions.

"Places!" she yelled.

Several dozen extras had been bused in earlier that morning and were now outfitted with villager costumes. They quickly assumed their positions, crowding around but not obscuring the figure of Shann.

"Okay. You've been having a festival of sorts," Jake instructed. "You've been dancing and drinking. Then this stranger, this off-worlder, interrupts you." He pointed to Paul Tortorella. "He pulls a weapon on you, and even though you don't know what it is, you sense danger.

"Shann is trying to take away the gun when he's interrupted by the great sorceress who lives on this mountain. Her powers make the weapon useless, and she tells everyone to hit the road. Follow Shann—Dion, that is. He'll lead you away, down the hillside. Understand?"

There were murmurs of assent as Jake pointed out marks on the ground indicating boundaries for the villagers. They gathered around Dion, who stood at the center of the clearing.

Admiring his appearance in his festival clothes—an open-necked brown leather tunic and pants painted with blue symbols and set off by a huge masculine necklace of bronze and blue stone pieces—Randi could believe she was looking at a beautiful, barbaric prince from some otherworldly culture. His bearing was proud and his expression strong and serious.

Randi had to admit that perhaps Olga had been right in her casting of the actor. So far she was pleased with Dion's filmed performance. And, thank goodness, he didn't seem determined to live his character every moment, as Nora did. Rather, he naturally assumed it. At least Randi *thought* she could distinguish between Dion's personality and that of Shann.

"They're ready," Jake said, leaping over a tree stump and making his way to Randi's side.

Laughing and dancing together in primitive abandon, the extras noisily acted out their scene until Paul appeared with the weapon. An expectant hush fell over the crowd at exactly the right moment. Approvingly Randi watched the scene smoothly unfold: Dion's struggle, the appearance of the sorceress and her instructions to leave.

Randi stopped the scene long enough to move the master camera for a reverse angle. Then she raced down the tree-covered hillside to the second camera unit so she could get the full impact of the crowd rushing toward them.

61

As the cameras rolled, Dion led the extras down the side of the mountain. Randi spotted mere glimpses of running villagers as the multitude fled through the underbrush.

"I think we're going to have to reshoot this," the cameraman muttered. "They look too far away."

"Something's wrong. You should have a clear shot of them."

"And where is all the rock coming from?"

Randi knit her brows as she watched a host of pebbles bounce their way from a copse of bushes and ping off the trunks of several trees. Larger, fist-size rocks followed. Then, accompanied by startled grunts and cries, so did several human bodies.

"What?" Randi cried.

It all happened so fast she had no time to stop either the action or the cameras. Helplessly she watched several more villagers careen from the undergrowth, sliding prone like human toboggans. A man picked himself up from under a tree and rubbed his head.

"What a ride!" he complained.

"What's going on here?" Randi shouted.

"He took them the wrong way! They've hit loose rock!" yelled Jake as he ran down the path toward her.

As Randi watched helplessly, the human landslide continued down the short, steep incline through the brush, accompanied by rocks, twigs and parts of torn costumes. Noisy chaos reigned. Some distance away Dion and three villagers emerged from the bush to watch the scene with amazement.

Randi couldn't believe the speed with which the unrehearsed scene began or ended, but as soon as she regained her senses, she was running toward the bedraggled people on the ground, some of whom lay quite still.

"I hope no one's seriously hurt," Jake said, panting beside her.

Randi kneeled beside a groaning woman. "Let me help you."

"I'm all right," the woman assured her. "I'll probably just be covered with bruises."

"I didn't know we were going to *fall* down the mountain," a man complained. "I would have dressed for the part—worn my football helmet."

Grimly Randi walked among the fallen extras, Jake and the crew's nurse joining her. After helping everyone up and carefully checking for injuries, Randi was relieved to find the fiasco had produced only one sprained ankle and a few dozen bruises and scratches.

They were lucky no one was seriously hurt, Randi thought. However, the production was going to be held up again. Before she could reshoot the scene, almost every costume would have to be repaired.

"How did this happen?" Jake asked her as they helped the extras limp away.

Dion walked ahead of them, carrying the woman with the sprained ankle.

"I don't know," said Randi, staring at the actor's back thoughtfully. "But I'm going to check it out."

"There are bad powers loose on this planet," intoned Nora ominously, her fingers nervously plucking at her arms. She opened her large blue eyes wide and peered around, a frightened expression on her face.

"Cut it out, Nora!" Randi insisted angrily. "Right now I can't deal with you as some spaced-out character." Randi glared fiercely into the actress's face. "Either get back to the real Nora or so help me, I'll see about committing you to the nearest mental institution!"

Nora looked stunned. "I . . . I'm only practicing for my part," she stammered.

"Well, save it for the filmed scenes—do your acting in front of the camera!"

"Okay." Gazing at Randi as if she were a monster, the actress quietly wandered off toward her own tent.

Randi left Jake in charge at the camp. Returning to their location, she quickly climbed the hillside. When she reached the marked boulder, she gazed down through the trees in the direction Dion was to have taken. The ground was obviously unmarked by hurrying extras' feet. Pulling herself higher, clutching shrub branches, Randi looked for the mistaken direction the group had taken.

Although there were similar boulders nearby, there should have been no mistake. Dion had been told to look for the rock marked with white paint. She could see it. Why hadn't he? The way he had led the extras obviously had not been clear enough to allow a rapid escape.

What was the matter with him? Was he deliberately trying to cause problems or was he just balking at taking directions? Randi stomped back down the incline, slowing when her foot dislodged a stone. She didn't want to roll down the mountain too. She intended to be in one piece when she faced Dion.

Late that night, walking among the extras as the nurse applied bandages and ointment, Randi felt like Scarlett O'Hara after the fall of the Confederate troops in *Gone with the Wind*. Unfortunately, the multiple tumble down the mountain was proving to have caused other unpleasant complications.

"Can't you do anything for this rash?" asked a man with a miserable expression.

"I'm sorry, Mr. Jackson. The first aid supplies contain only a limited amount of lotion," the nurse answered. "We didn't expect forty-eight people to roll through poison oak."

"I've sent some of the crew to the nearest town to pick up more lotion," Randi told the man reassuringly.

"In the meantime, I guess I'll have to stand it," said Mr. Jackson, holding his arms away from his body awkwardly like a large bird. "Maybe I can focus on something else—women, booze, food." He sighed deeply. "Naw, I still itch."

As the man hobbled away bowlegged, the nurse whispered to Randi, "That guy is the worst of the lot. His pants were torn off!"

Randi shook her head sympathetically. "Well, at least he still has a sense of humor." Then, looking around, she asked, "Have you seen Dion?"

"He was here awhile ago," the nurse answered, "trying to help out by making poultices of his herbal tea. But we even ran out of that."

"I hope our emergency crew comes back fast," Randi said before striding away. Dusk was falling, and the camp lanterns were being lit. She headed for the commissary area. Two women were sitting near the main cook tent, their backs to her. At first Randi didn't recognize them.

"Can you believe it?" It was Sally Brown's voice. "Jake told me he saw Dion coming out of Ms. St. Martin's tent the other night. Really!" Sally laughed excitedly. "I know Dion has a reputation for establishing close relationships with his directors, but he's never been *this* close before!"

Clearing her throat, Randi stepped into the lantern

light so Sally would know she'd overheard. Filled with anger, she stared at the woman and was gratified to see her look uncomfortable.

"Um, hello, Randi," Sally said, smiling too widely.

Not deigning to answer, Randi stalked off. Had she been right in assuming that Jake had been the one spreading gossip about her to the network? It certainly seemed likely, with Sally quoting him and repeating rumors. Although Randi realized that kind of backstabbing was rampant in Hollywood, she had hoped Sally had more class. Randi had thought she could be friendly with the other woman, at least on a professional basis. Now she would make it a point to avoid her.

When she neared the group of tables on the far side of the commissary tent, Randi spotted Dion bending over one of the female extras.

"Just follow Dr. Dion's orders," he said as Randi came up behind him. "Keep applying this."

The young girl beamed at him. "Oh, thank you, Mr. Hayden. I feel so much better already! This is so exciting, even if we did have an accident!"

"Excuse me," Randi said. "Do you suppose I could talk to Dr. Dion alone?"

With a surprised and not too happy look, the girl rose and slipped away.

"Why didn't you kiss it and make it well?" suggested Randi sarcastically. "Or give her a back rub? She'll probably dream of you anyway."

Did Dion play doctor with all his women? Randi's eyes narrowed, and Dion frowned in response.

"Look, I'm sorry this fiasco happened. I made a terrible mistake and somehow managed to take everyone the wrong way."

"So, you think you can just say you're sorry and go on as if nothing happened?"

"I was going to find you to explain, but I've been so busy trying to help out with the mess, I haven't had time to look for you. This is the first chance I've had to sit down since the accident."

Randi looked at the cup of wine and plate of food on the table in front of him. "You're going to eat and drink and call it a day?"

All at once Randi became aware of her own hunger. She hadn't eaten since morning. She looked longingly at the sandwich on Dion's plate. With all the day's problems, she couldn't believe she was actually thinking of food. She was dieting anyway!

"Is there something else I can do?" he asked.

"Try being responsible. Listen to directions."

Dion looked surprised. "I listened to your directions, Randi. I just happened to see the wrong big rock with white marks on it. It was a mistake, but an easy one to make! I'm lucky I didn't fall with the other actors."

"You're always lucky." Randi's palms were starting to itch. Absentmindedly she began to scratch them. "Other people suffer, but you never seem to."

"Now wait a minute. Let's not blow the situation out of perspective." Dion's mobile features hardened into a mask. "If it makes you feel better, I suppose I could go and toss myself down the incline too."

"Why don't you?"

"Are you serious?"

"I just wish you'd do something besides charm your way through life making money and showing off your profile."

"I'm not exactly making a fortune doing this miniseries!"

"I'm aware of that, and it surprises me. Why are you here?" The thought came out of nowhere, but it seemed to fit the situation. "To sabotage me?"

"You're getting as paranoid as Nora. Next you'll accuse me of being from outer space." Then, seriously, he told her, "I'm doing *Chrysalis* because I want to. I really don't have to worry about money now."

"How nice for you."

"Wait just a minute," Dion countered. "I may be lucky, but I prepared myself for a role like this one. I've taken enough acting lessons to have a degree in the subject. And why would I want to sabotage you? I suppose I could come up with some reason, considering the way you acted toward me in the past, but I don't hold grudges."

"I don't know what you're talking about."

"I always wondered why you were so tough on me. I think you had some emotions tied up with your cool mental processes."

"What are you suggesting?"

"I think we've been attracted to each other from the first time we met. You just don't want to admit it."

"Oh, really? And you like tough women?"

"I admire the tough professional I recognize in you, and I like the soft woman underneath." Dion stepped nearer. "There's fire beneath that cool surface. . . ."

Randi seethed. "I came to discuss your mistake. I'm in no mood to have a personal discussion with you." She gestured emphatically with both hands, then realized he was staring at them.

"What's wrong with your hands?"

Not knowing what he was talking about, she looked at them. Red welts crisscrossed the fleshy areas.

"You've got it too."

"Great! Just what I need!"

Randi kept staring at her hands as if the ailment would disappear. A subtle itching seemed to radiate from the core of her flesh.

"I still have a little of a tea poultice left." Dion put an arm around Randi's shoulders and drew her over to the table. He took a bag from a cup and with it rubbed the cool liquid over her hands. "Now don't touch any other part of your body or you'll spread it."

Looking up into his face, Randi realized she could spread the rash to someone else, too. She was highly tempted.

"My poor Foxy. That must be terribly uncomfortable." His concerned tone got to her, and Randi had a hard time hanging on to her anger as Dion told her, "I know how it feels. I had poison ivy a few years ago."

"You actually had a physical ailment?"

"I'm human."

"Surprising. Rumor says you're a god."

"Don't believe everything you read. I suffer like everyone else," he assured her. "Even emotionally. You used to make me suffer a lot when we worked on *Wrangler.*"

"What's that supposed to mean?"

"I was a sitcom actor thrown into the big league, and you wanted Academy Award material on the first try."

"I wasn't the director!" Randi's goodwill was fading fast. She bristled at the criticism. "I was only carrying out his orders."

"Something may have been lost in the interpretation."

"That's not fair! I always thought very carefully before I issued any kind of direction."

"If you'd listened to your emotions instead of your 'cool mental processes . . .' "

"I'd have harmed you physically a long time ago."

Extricating herself from Dion's grasp without touching him with her infected hands, Randi strode off to her tent.

The emergency lotion supply for the poison oak arrived in the early hours of the morning. Randi was relieved when she heard the jeep pull in. Maybe now she could get some real sleep.

By that time Randi was stretched out on her sleeping bag, holding her arms in an awkward position in front of her, hands covered in thin white cotton gloves normally used when handling or editing film. She had been trying to forget the itch that was plaguing her.

Before retiring well after midnight, Randi had made one last check on the suffering extras who were resting uncomfortably in their tents. There had been nothing more that she had been able to do for them but offer words of encouragement. If they didn't scratch themselves and thereby spread the rash, it should be gone in a few days.

Randi herself was more than physically uncomfortable. Her thoughts seemed to whirl through the darkness into which she stared. Why couldn't she forget about Dion and his questionable claims about their working together on *Wrangler?* Had she been too tough on him? Randi was sure she hadn't treated him any different than the other actors. Had she?

But what if she had distorted her view of the way things were? No! Randi definitely remembered Dion's temper tantrums on the set. Those had been real enough. Regardless of what she might have done, there was no excuse for them.

Randi sighed. But how could Dion act so differently now? Had he cleverly learned to hide a serious character flaw? It simply didn't make sense.

Listening to the sounds beyond her tent of muted voices and scufflings, she knew the extras were receiving the lotion. Randi struggled to rise from her bedroll.

She refused to think about Dion and their differing opinions any longer. At the moment she intended to get some relief for her hands so she could sleep soundly until sunrise. There was a lot of work to do the next day, and *Chrysalis* was Randi's main concern.

CHAPTER FIVE

"Randi, should we finish loading the mules and horses or what?" Jake demanded to know.

"With everything but bodies," Randi agreed. "It's too hot to have everyone mounted and waiting for me while I finish stuffing my backpack."

Jake inspected his watch and shook his neatly cropped head of light brown hair before turning to speak to the head wrangler. With a resentful glance at his back, Randi headed for the bus, jamming on her western hat to shade her eyes. So what if they were a few hours behind schedule getting on the trail? Did Jake think he had something worth reporting back to the network?

Still not sure her assistant director was the spy in their midst, Randi didn't know who'd be a better suspect. How else would the network boys have known to check out the dailies of the poison oak fiasco if Jake hadn't told them about it? Benny was still prattling about that disaster!

Glancing around the pack station in the Giant Forest area of Sequoia National Park, Randi was gratified to note that everything finally looked organized. She'd been busy during the early morning hours making sure their departure went smoothly; therefore, she hadn't had a chance to transfer clothes from her suitcases to a backpack.

Almost everyone in the cast and crew was on the road back to Los Angeles. With the main portion of *Chrysalis* already in the can, only a half-dozen cast members and a dozen or so others would be heading for their next location higher in the Sierras. By necessity, they were forced to travel light.

"Need any help, Foxy?"

Startled, Randi looked up to see Dion, his shapely, denim-clad hip anchored against a tree scant yards from the bus. His arms were crossed over his chest, hiding much of the skin exposed by his open blue work shirt. A sweat-stained Stetson covered his hair. Hardly the golden god image, she thought sourly.

"You'd only distract me. Why don't you go over to the loading area to keep the troops entertained?"

Dion's laughter was softened by the thickly padded forest floor. "I'd rather entertain the general. Privately."

That was all she'd need to start the gossip spreading again!

"I don't have time, Dion," she said, briskly walking past him and up the steps into the bus. "Sorry."

Quickly repacking, Randi heard Dion whistling. He wasn't budging from that tree! She stuffed the already bulging sack with a vengeance, then turned to fill her briefcase. She scooped up a pile of papers she'd left on her seat, part script pages, part notes to herself.

The stack almost slipped from her hands. Randi recovered everything but the carefully folded front page of a tabloid, which fluttered from the pile, reminding her of Benny's visit to the set the evening before.

Now all Randi could see were the boldface words

73

GOLDEN GOD and underneath IN BED OF, but she vividly remembered the headline: GOLDEN GOD FINDS INSPIRATION IN BED OF WOMAN DIRECTOR. The story went on to say how Hollywood idol Dion Hayden had first-time director Randi St. Martin right where he wanted her.

"Hah! What do they know?" she muttered, stuffing the paper into a zippered pocket of her backpack. She should have had as much fun as the article claimed!

Who was responsible for the fraudulent exposé? she wondered. The story seemed to be based on that night Jake saw Dion leaving her tent. But that had been weeks ago. Randi wondered if Dion had seen the tabloid yet. She certainly wasn't about to show him the trashy blurb.

"Hey, General St. Martin, time to leave your trench. The demolition squad is here," Dion informed her from the entryway.

Randi saw the bus driver heading their way. He was ready to take the bus and the extra gear they couldn't bring along back to the studio. Grabbing her things and exiting, she was surprised when Dion took the pack from her.

"Let me be a gentleman, would you?"

"A new part for you?"

Noting Dion's scowl, Randi felt a twinge of guilt. That poor excuse for journalism wasn't his fault. They were both victims, even if gossip didn't seem to bother Dion. But then his career wasn't on the line.

"Can we declare a truce?" Dion asked.

Randi nodded. "I never did like war."

He seemed to accept her backhanded apology. They walked to the loading area in silence, but Randi was completely aware of the man beside her and the feelings he

74

always stirred up. She'd have to be dead not to be attracted to Dion Hayden.

"You can tell everyone to start mounting," Randi told Jake as a wrangler tied her briefcase and backpack to one of the dozen mules that made up the pack train.

"Our horses are over there," Dion said, leading the way.

Eyeing her dark mount suspiciously—could she trust a horse with the name Diablo?—Randi wondered if she was up to the experience of spending two or more weeks in the wilderness on horseback. Realizing she'd stall all day if she could find a way, she patted her horse on the nose and grabbed the reins.

"Here goes."

"I'll give you a leg up," a warm voice suggested from behind her.

"I can get on myself." The words were spoken with more assurance than she felt.

Threading her fingers through the reins and grabbing the horse's mane, she lifted a booted foot and barely got her toe through the high stirrup. She couldn't seem to get the leverage necessary to spring into the saddle, and now, hopping but getting nowhere, she was making her mount nervous.

Snorting loudly, Diablo eyed her with suspicion. Randi was about to look for a rock to use as a mounting block when she felt Dion's firm hands around her waist. Each finger left a sizzling imprint through the light cotton of her turquoise western shirt.

"Don't fight it."

This time when Randi bounced upward, she hefted herself into the saddle easily, yet she was left breathless.

"Thanks."

"No problem. I remember you weren't overly thrilled with horses when we shot *Wrangler.*"

"Riding's never been my favorite sport," she admitted. "I never learned to control a horse too well."

"And a tough lady like you is nervous when she doesn't have complete control," Dion softly suggested as he mounted a palomino named Olympia.

Randi grinned. "You know me better than I thought you did."

"It's about time you realized that."

As Sam, the head wrangler, led the way out single file, Randi's concentration on her riding was broken both by the sight of Dion on his mare directly in front of her and by the spectacle of scenery surrounding them.

On the "Big Trees," cinnamon-colored bark fluted like hand-carved Grecian columns rose more than two hundred feet high. These giant sequoias were the largest living things on earth, their trunks measuring as much as forty feet in diameter. Randi lost her sense of proportion as she gazed into the branches high overhead. Heavy and twisted, they tapered into puffs of delicate evergreen far away in the Mediterranean blue sky. She could fancy them being created by the ancient gods, for some were more than three thousand years old.

"Isn't this real! We're at one with nature. How inspiring!"

Randi's thoughts were interrupted by Nora's loud squeal as she trotted by, flopping up and down in her saddle with tooth-jarring regularity.

"You're not going to think so tonight when you try to sit down," Paul predicted darkly, keeping his horse right behind hers. "Now get back in line. This is supposed to be single file so the horses don't get ideas!"

"Gee, what kind of ideas could a horse get?" Randi heard the actress ask as she followed Paul's instructions. "I wonder what it would be like to be a horse."

The thought was punctuated by a very loud but human neigh. Did that mean Nora planned to practice the Technique as a horse? Randi wondered. She heard Dion's low-throated chuckle ahead of her. Randi was certainly glad he didn't carry the acting method into his everyday life.

In spite of two short rest stops, Randi was ready to call it quits long before their caravan arrived at their camp for the night. She was tired and achy and knew there was worse to come. She'd kept herself entertained by switching focus back and forth from Dion's broad shoulders and trim waist to the ever-changing scenery, but now she wanted the comfort of solid ground under her feet.

Not trusting horses in the first place, Randi found it highly disconcerting to be on Diablo's pitching back, listening to his iron shoes slip and grate halfway up a steep incline. She made a major mistake by looking straight down the cliff along which they traveled. Far below, the trees diminished and seemed like mere blades of grass underneath them. How far was down, anyway? Randi wondered as Diablo slipped, then regained his footing. A light sweat broke out over her body.

"Hang on a second," Randi called over her shoulder to Jocelyn so the expert rider wouldn't run over her. "I'm getting off and walking."

As she began to dismount, Dion turned his horse to approach her. "I don't think you should try to walk, Randi. The horse is used to this trail. You're not."

His expression was mildly disapproving, which only made Randi more determined to do as she pleased. Irritation and fear almost prompted her to suggest that Dion

77

ride his horse over the cliff, but Randi stopped the words from forming. He was concerned. She couldn't fault him for that.

Forcing a tired smile to her lips, she said, "Thanks, but I've got to try. I'm getting large doses of vertigo every time one of Diablo's hooves slips on the stone."

"I'll ride next to you, then. Give me Diablo's reins."

Dion led her horse and talked. He was trying to keep her calm, Randi thought, but she didn't have enough energy to carry on a conversation and keep her balance too. When she finally lost her footing altogether, she went down hard on her hands and knees, and loose stones splayed in every direction.

"Damn!"

Dion was at her side in a flash. "Are you hurt?"

Rising, Randi looked at her palms. "Not really. I only scraped my hands."

"Poor Foxy. And they just healed a few days ago too."

Randi sighed. "I guess you were right. Diablo is used to this; I'm not."

Without saying the expected "I told you so," Dion offered her a handkerchief to wipe her palms, then helped her remount. To Randi's relief, it wasn't much farther to their campsite. She felt like a mess as she awkwardly slid from Diablo's back when they got there, and she couldn't help but notice how fresh and glamorous Jocelyn seemed as she gracefully dismounted.

The wranglers were experienced and efficient, and with the help of Dion, Jake and Chuck Brockman, camp was set up quickly. Randi helped unload a few of the mules.

"How soon till chow?" she heard Paul ask Sam.

"Probably an hour or so."

"I'm hungry now!"

78

"So am I. We could go berry picking," Nora offered.

"*You* can go berry picking," Paul said. "But watch out for the bears."

"Bears?" Nora looked around. "Sam, are there really bears here?"

"Yes, ma'am. But don't be afraid," the wrangler told her. "You just have to use your head. Don't leave food around. That's what attracts 'em. We tie supplies in plastic bags and hang them from trees with bear cables." He wagged a cautioning finger at her. "If you find them berries, don't bring any in your tent tonight."

"Forget it," Nora said. "I really don't like berries anyway."

"I'm going for a walk," Randi told Nora. "Maybe it'll straighten out my saddle-bowed legs."

A quick glance around the camp assured her Dion was nowhere to be seen. Part of her was relieved that she'd finally be alone, but as she started off down the trail she recognized a small longing to have Dion beside her.

How tranquil it was among the red firs, with their purplish red bark and long purple cones. Randi was enjoying her solitude. Glancing at her palms, she thought of Dion and the gentle way he'd inspected the scrapes.

Could he really have become a different person in three years? she wondered as she walked farther from camp. His acting had improved. He no longer had tantrums on the set. But those were superficial changes. He was kind and caring . . . but perhaps he always had been. Perhaps all he'd needed was time to mature.

But had Dion been justified in accusing her of being too tough on him? Randi had thought about it for the past week.

At nineteen Dion had been the rising star of Hollywood after being given the lead role in a television sitcom, the decision based solely on his projected appeal to teenage girls. Then several years later he'd been given a lead in *Wrangler,* his first movie. Yes, the dream had been placed on a silver platter and handed to a young man with neither experience nor natural talent, and Randi St. Martin had resented the fact, knowing how hard she had worked to get where she was. She had seen her parents sacrifice their ideals, values and private lives to chase their dream. They'd made it, but at what price? Determined to beat the system with its glorification of glamour and violence, with its drug deals, casting couches and devious pressure tactics, Randi had, indeed, learned to be tough.

Still, Randi wasn't convinced she'd been unfair to Dion, but she admitted he'd been right about something else: She'd wanted him from the first time she met him.

A rustling interrupted her reverie, and Randi paused. There it was again. An animal moving through the undergrowth? Nothing small made that much noise, Randi decided. She'd better get back to camp. There was only one problem: which direction?

Randi struck off to the right and was disconcerted when the animal seemed to follow. Her heart thudding, she glanced around, but in the gloom of the forest, details dropped off sharply. She couldn't see anything. What could be following her? A bear!

Her mouth went dry. Running now, she wasn't sure which way to go. Lost, with a bear on her trail! For one insane second Randi thought of climbing the nearest tree, then realized any bear could climb better and faster than she!

A murmuring ahead assured her she was going in the

right direction, but when Randi broke through the copse of firs into a clearing, her heart dropped. She'd heard running water, not voices. Standing on a ledge, she stared at a small waterfall starting some yards above, rushing to a stream below. And the noise was closer. Did bears swim?

Tears pricked her eyelids. Should she jump? Pulse throbbing, Randi edged closer to the precipice, ready to make a last-minute escape. The crashing sounds rose to a crescendo. She looked down into the foaming water swirling around several large rocks. Randi closed her eyes and bent her knees.

"Hey, Randi! What are you doing?"

"Dion!" she croaked.

In her relief, Randi's knees gave way, but Dion was there to catch her in his arms. She clung to him, fingers digging into the flesh of his biceps.

"I thought you were a bear."

"What? And no doubt you were thinking of jumping to get away?"

When she nodded, he squeezed her tight. "Oh, Randi, you must really have been frightened. I don't know what I would have done if you'd been hurt. But it's all right now," he murmured. "I'm here."

Instantly Randi tried to steady herself and push Dion away. "I'm fine."

"No you're not." He pulled her back to the wall of his chest and wrapped his arms around her. "You're still shaking. Stop trying to be so tough all the time."

"Self-sufficient," she corrected him, but Randi had lost the urge to stand on her own. His arms were so comforting, and something within her gave over to the unfamiliar but peculiarly soothing feeling of being protected.

81

Dion wedged her head into the hollow between his neck and shoulder and stroked her hair. Randi realized she'd wrapped her arms around him, and her fingers were splayed across his back, the tips sensitized to the texture of his coarse work shirt and the heat of his flesh beneath it. Her heart still thudded strongly, but Randi knew it was no longer out of fright.

"Everyone is entitled to a soft side, my lovely Ariadne," Dion whispered into her hair. "Being soft is not the same as being weak. I know you're a strong person. I love that about you." His words seemed to echo off the rocks and mingle with the pleasant sounds of the waterfall behind them. He kissed the top of her head and rested his cheek there. "But can't you save your tough exterior for your profession and remember you're a woman once in a while? We all have personal needs, but you ignore yours. I'd like to help you take care of them."

"I—I'm not sure," Randi whispered, afraid once more.

His fingers trailed through her hair and down her spine, a gesture both tender and erotic. Randi could feel the increased beat of Dion's pulse where her cheek lay nestled against him. She hoped he spoke from the heart. Responding to his enticing words, Randi became pliant and devoid of resistance.

She was no longer the director, he the actor. They were two people who needed each other, at least for the moment. Randi allowed herself to be the woman he sought, yet she couldn't find the words to tell him so.

When he drew back, she was disappointed, for the warmth of his splendid body was addicting. But Dion had no intention of letting Randi go. He only moved far enough away to tilt back her head and stare into her face.

Her body still lay against his, sweetly warmed from breasts to thighs.

Randi wished Dion would kiss her.

"You have such beautiful russet eyes," Dion whispered, his face inches from hers. "They're honest, just like the woman. They tell me everything I want to know."

"Such as?" she asked breathlessly.

"They tell me you want me to kiss you."

Randi watched as his face moved closer with agonizing slowness. She studied his eyes, their blue intensified by his passion. Then her gaze dropped and she memorized every inch of his sun-kissed skin along the way to his sculpted mouth.

Just before his lips touched hers, everything went into soft focus, perhaps the way she'd film such a scene in a movie, a love scene between two people who had waited a long, long time for this moment.

A hazy wide shot would expose the beauty of the setting: stately fir trees swaying in the wind, their graceful movement counterbalanced by the hard solidity of the mountain on which the lovers stood; the last tiger lilies of late summer gently nodding their speckled orange heads as the lovers embraced; the sparkling waterfall tumbling over rocks, hinting of rainbows and precious treasures.

The first kiss would be deep and lingering, the light-headed excitement of two sensual natures displayed by sweeping around the lovers: trees a blur of green behind them, mixing and blending with dark earth tones; a crystal cascade transformed into brilliant orange-red flames of a setting sun; russet waves tossed and mingled with golden curls.

The lovers would remain the center of focus, the camera finally moving in to capture their loveplay in close-up: his hands moving around her hips and up her torso to lightly linger at her breasts; her hands unbuckling her belt, giving him leave to take her; their fingers touching and tugging, removing barriers until flesh met flesh.

But the erotic mental storyboard couldn't match the reality before her eyes: Dion, the only man who refused to be banished from her memory.

As Randi stood naked on a windswept precipice in the middle of a mountain wilderness, so her more vulnerable inner being was equally exposed. Opening herself to Dion, she silently bade he use her gently. The promise that he would lingered in his eyes.

A tender stroke from her cheek to her ear made her shiver in response. Dion's fingertips trailing down her neck began a quiet explosion, a chain reaction spreading to each eager nerve in her body. Randi breathlessly waited to see what he would offer, allowing him to direct their lovemaking for the moment.

Dion caressed her, tracing every part of her, lingering intimately at her breasts. Flushing, Randi felt her body respond, swelling and melting simultaneously. His approval was apparent in the intensity of his gaze.

This time he used both hands, lightly cupping her cheeks and seeking her lips with his own. And while his tongue investigated the mysteries of her mouth, his fingers explored the lush secrets of her body.

Dion teased her breasts, finding her nipples with his thumbs. He stroked them to agonizing peaks, until Randi moaned aloud. At the sound she felt a warm stirring against her belly and remembered how much his pleasure had been intensified by her own on that one night they had shared.

Her fingers reached up, finding delight in his curls. His hands slid down and did likewise. With insistent pressure he eased open her thighs with one hand while capturing her buttocks with the other. Then he began a sensual foray, his fingers finding and seeking shelter, his pleasure becoming hers.

"Dion!" The word exploded into his mouth.

"What is it, Randi? Tell me what you want."

"You!"

Randi nuzzled the crook of Dion's neck and hung on to his hair as he bent her pliant body to the cool rock below. But all the while he continued to touch and tease, discovering the innermost secrets of her body with his wickedly wonderful fingers.

Her thighs opened and bade him enter, yet he wasn't through with his delicious torture. He tantalized the sensitive flesh between her thighs until she ached with need. Wanting to wait no longer, Randi found and guided him until he was lost within her.

Dion shuddered and pulled his chest away so they were joined only from the waist down. He studied her face intently while moving with agonizing slowness, and Randi felt herself flush under his tender scrutiny.

Aware of the hard, cool surface against her back, breathing in the fragrant scent of dry wood and pine, Randi felt at one with the earth and all of nature while Dion coaxed the most primeval of responses from her. She stared, fascinated with the man above her.

Running a hand up his chest, scraping her nails through the sprinkling of pale curls, Randi fancied him as her own golden god.

He was perfection, a composite of masculine beauty and grace attributed to the deities of the ancient worlds.

She touched his cheek, explored the finely chiseled features that had haunted so many of her dreams. Dion seared the inside of her wrist with the moistness of his tongue. Shivering with delight, Randi studied Dion's eyes and imagined herself floating in a Mediterranean sky.

A teasing wind challenged the waterfall and misted their bodies with its damp embrace, but the chilly water only served to intensify the flames of Randi's burning passion. She thrust her hips at Dion, silently demanding he quench the fire blazing within her.

Dion broke the thread of their gaze, dipping his head to her breast. Randi arched, eager to feel his tongue and teeth against her flesh. It only took one small nip to tighten and intensify the coiling sensation deep inside. She hadn't meant to voice the silent moan that echoed in her mind, but it escaped her throat in an agonized rush.

"Oh, Dion!"

The movement against her hips paused for a second—it seemed as if an eternity passed while Randi hung suspended between heaven and earth—when Dion lifted his head to look into her face.

"Randi!" he whispered, and plunging deeply into her, he began to shudder.

Everything blurred into soft focus as Randi's body followed Dion's path to ecstasy, but even as she trembled under him, she knew no film could capture the fulfillment she experienced.

After Dion kissed her sweetly, he rested his damp forehead against hers so their noses pressed together. He lay over her but kept his weight on his elbows and knees. When Randi trailed her nails down his spine, he wriggled and made sexy noises of approval that were so exaggerated she had to laugh.

"I like that sound," Dion murmured. "Like a whisper of wind chimes in the fluttering breeze."

"How poetic," Randi teased.

"I'd love to write poems to you." Dion attempted to kiss her without removing his forehead or nose from hers but only succeeded in smacking the air a hair's-breadth from her mouth. "Let's see. How about this:

> There once was a lady from Hollywood,
> Who always made films that were very good.
> But when she undressed . . .
> She was the best of the best . . .
> And she'd be even better if she could!"

Pushing Dion over onto his side, Randi poked his chest in mock outrage. "That's a lusty limerick, not a poem!"

"I guess that means I'm a lusty actor, not a poet." Dion poked her in return, but in a clever way that made Randi catch her breath. "Tch-tch. Your mouth is open. I'll have to fix that."

Dion swooped over her, attacking her mouth while rolling in the direction of the cascade. Randi landed on top, her lips still affixed to his, Dion's firm hand holding her head in place.

"Mdslstlwysmkuzly?"

Dion let go of her head. "What?"

"I asked if lust always made you silly."

Dion kissed Randi gently and ran his thumb across her cheek. "No, but being happy does."

Gazing into his smiling face, Randi felt a strange tightness at the back of her throat. It was an awkward moment, filled with questions, perhaps ones better left unasked, the antithesis of their loveplay of a moment ago.

"Stop thinking and enjoy," Dion ordered softly.

He cuddled her, and Randi was peculiarly content. Closing her eyes, she did enjoy the feel of his hand smoothing her hair. She snuggled closer, absorbing Dion's warmth as protection from the now chilly evening air. Her hand trailed downward and slipped between their bodies to stroke him to renewed life.

Then the breeze shifted again, carrying with it cold spray from the falls.

"A-ah!" Randi screeched as they were drenched.

"That sure cooled you off quickly," Dion said with a chuckle.

"Go ahead, laugh." Randi was already shivering as she tried to cover herself while moving toward her clothes. "You're as wet as I am, and it's darn cold!"

Dion got his hands on the clothing first. "Oh, no. They're damp too." He helped her into her clothes, then climbed into his own. "Better?"

"Yes," Randi admitted. "But let's get back before the temperature drops even more." She paused and stared at Dion. "Uh, you do know the way back, don't you?"

"Trust me."

Could she trust him? Randi wondered as they walked hand in hand through the silent firs. Pushing damp tendrils of hair out of her eyes, Randi decided she didn't want to think about anything but the present. Their lovemaking had been a wonderful experience, so why spoil it by remembering the past or doubting the future?

Dion released her hand shortly before they broke into the clearing and headed for the campfire, a beacon in the deepening darkness. Randi was sure everyone was staring at their bedraggled appearance.

"It's about time you two got back," Jake said, raising an eyebrow. "We were beginning to wonder if we should send out a rescue team."

"But we should have known you'd be all right together," Sally added, and Randi was sure the other woman knew exactly how all right and how together they had been.

Randi simply didn't care. Let everyone gossip to their hearts' content, she thought defiantly as she and Dion helped themselves to supper. Rumors had been rampant before anything had transpired between them. How much more harm could be done?

Sitting on the same log with Dion, Randi couldn't help but wonder what he was thinking. Although he smiled tenderly at her, he was so quiet. Why? Was it because he was already sorry they'd made love or because he'd satisfied his lusty appetite? Annoyed with herself, Randi quickly ate twice as much as she normally would. What was done was done, and she didn't want to go back to change what had happened at the waterfall.

"Hey, Randi, want a roasted marshmallow?" Nora called from the campfire. "M-m-m. I mean they're where it's at, all crisp and brown but gooey inside."

"Yeah, soft like some people's heads," Paul muttered, but the words had an affectionate ring. Nora ignored him and held out her marshmallow stick toward Randi.

"Thanks, Nora."

Threading the stick with two marshmallows, Randi held it over the fire. When she glanced back to ask Dion if he wanted one, his spot on the log was vacant. Too close to the blaze, the marshmallows caught fire, reminding Randi of the one Dion had started in her such a short time ago.

Sighing as she blew out the flames, Randi knew she needed to be realistic. In spite of her past and present reservations about Dion, she had opened herself to the charming actor. What would he offer her in return?

More important, what did she really want from him?

CHAPTER SIX

It was dawn when Randi awoke, and the dim interior of her tent was as gray as her half-remembered dreams.

Dreams! She struggled to extricate herself from the blanket that was now entangling her feet in intricate folds inside the sleeping bag. What a night she'd had!

It had started with the chorus of wolves—no, coyotes, Randi silently amended. At moonrise, after everyone in the camp had retired, she'd awakened to the nearby howling of a lone coyote. His solo had been answered first by one, then another of the beasts until the camp seemed surrounded by an eerie concert of yips and cries. Randi had imagined the animals circling as she'd listened. The din had gone on for at least an hour, keeping her from sleeping.

Then, after she'd finally drifted off, her slumber had been restless. She'd dreamed of running through a dark forest of endless, towering trees in which she'd been searching for Dion. Alone, she ran on and on, seeming to have no control over her legs. Randi had been terrified, because no matter how far or how fast she ran, she hadn't been able to find Dion.

And what if she had found him?

Randi shivered as she scrambled from her warm bedroll to pull on a flannel shirt, jeans and boots. Would finding Dion have frightened her more? After they'd made wonderful love a few evenings before, Randi had thrown herself into her work. It would be easy for her to admit she felt some kind of attraction that went beyond a one-night stand. But where would it go from there? How could she predict what Dion would do next?

Randi didn't want to be dependent on any man, especially not on a glamorous and probably unreliable man like Dion. What pain she would feel if, growing addicted to his presence, she reached out in the night and there was no one to touch.

Opening the tent flap and pulling on her jacket in the bracing morning air, Randi headed for the cookfire located in the center of the camp. She quickly scanned the area, but Randi saw only the lone figure of the head wrangler crouched at the fire. With a heavy stick, he poked at the charred wood until flames shot up into the early morning sky.

Where was Dion? Randi wondered, then admonished herself for thinking of him.

"Want some coffee?" the wrangler asked.

"Sure." She walked stiffly across the clearing.

"Oatmeal's ready too. You'll have to wait for the bacon and eggs."

Eyes blurry, feeling unsettled, Randi wondered if she should indulge her appetite. Food could ease the hollow feeling with which she'd awakened.

"How about an order of eggs Florentine and some freshly squeezed orange juice?" Paul Tortorella asked as he joined Randi at the fire. "Guess I'm going to have to complain about the chow when we get down the mountain. How do they expect us to work without luxuries?"

92

Randi looked at Paul and met his grin. She realized he was joking, which was unusual behavior for him.

"I know, I know. We're lucky to be able to cart anything up into this godforsaken wilderness," Paul said, heaping oatmeal into a bowl. "I guess it is pretty desolate up here."

Randi looked beyond the few firs bordering their new campsite higher in the Sierra Mountains. Gazing into the distance, she could see the end of the timberline where the land was open, often steeply inclined and rocky. Any trees growing in that high country resembled strangely formed creepers, hanging low in order to avoid the sixty-mile-an-hour winds.

"It sure is surreal-looking." Paul seemed to be trying to get some sort of early-morning conversation going.

"Perfect for the home of a sorceress," Randi said, referring to the scenes they'd filmed the day before. As she watched, the sunrise tipped the jagged, austere peaks above them with silver and gold.

"Have some breakfast," Sam said.

Randi willingly took the plate of scrambled eggs the wrangler handed her.

"Where is everybody?" Paul asked. "The smell of food usually drags them out of the tents. Except for Jocelyn, of course." The model-turned-actress had a habit of sleeping late and skipping meals. "And no doubt Chuck Brockman is already out hiking."

"Good morning!" Nora's words were definitely on the positive side—a little odd for her this time of day. Pushing her blond hair from her eyes, Nora smiled sweetly at Paul and helped herself to a piece of bacon from his plate. "Do you mind?" she asked.

"Whatever makes you happy," Paul answered in a husky tone that made Randi stare.

The two actors were gazing at one another with friendly familiarity, looks she'd never seen pass between them before. Something was definitely going on. Had Nora come from the direction of Paul's tent?

Grabbing a biscuit with jelly and a cup of steaming coffee, Nora wriggled herself onto the rock next to Paul. With an intimate smile, Nora offered him part of her bread.

Well, Randi decided, she would no longer have to be concerned about tension between those two—unless they got into a lovers' quarrel. When had they made peace? Now that she thought about it, Randi realized there had been subtle changes in the actors' personalities during the last few days. For the better, thank goodness.

As she watched Paul place his arm around Nora's slender shoulders, the hollow feeling in Randi returned. Quickly she ate several bites of food, then tossed her paper plate into the nearby trash can. Eating a lot at breakfast just made her hungrier the rest of the day.

"This food's going to get cold," the wrangler grumbled. "Maybe the high altitude's making everyone too tired to get up."

"I'll wake Jocelyn," Nora offered, heading toward the lead actress's tent. "And here comes Naomi."

The older woman who played the sorceress joined the group at the fire.

Randi wondered if she should go to Dion's tent. She imagined seeing him asleep, his long lashes shadowing his high cheekbones. She would have to steel herself to resist his body's awakening warmth, made vulnerable and lethargic from the night's rest. Even if it had been three years since she'd slept next to him, Randi still remembered how tempting Dion had been in the morning.

Just as Randi put her coffee cup down, Dion's tent flap opened, but it wasn't Dion who emerged. It was Jake. He had an odd look on his face. Behind him came Sally Brown, her arms clutched tightly to her sweatered chest. There were circles beneath the woman's eyes, and the corners of her mouth were turned down. As Jake headed toward the fire and ignored Randi, Sally retreated in the opposite direction.

What was going on?

Finally Dion came out of the tent. Straightening and stretching, he met Randi's eyes and gave her a half-smile. Walking slowly to the cookfire, he poured himself some coffee and looked again at her.

Randi was nonplussed as she walked back to the fire and picked up a cup of coffee. Had some kind of meeting taken place in Dion's tent at dawn, a meeting about which she knew nothing? Had they been talking about her?

Still suspicious of Jake, having heard Sally's gossip with her own ears, Randi couldn't help but wonder. And what did Dion have to do with them? Was there a conspiracy among the three?

Patiently she waited for Dion to start a conversation, but he ate without looking at her.

"Well, I guess we're about ready to head for location," Randi announced, trying to sound enthusiastic.

"Okay," Dion said as he quickly ate the rest of his food.

His startlingly blue eyes met hers, but Randi couldn't read their expression. Had the electricity between them disappeared, or was Randi's imagination working too hard?

"See you at the lake," Dion said before he walked away.

Randi watched his retreating back and thought about the last few days of filming. In spite of her preoccupation with her job and the long hours, she'd noticed that Dion had kept a friendly distance. Randi secretly had been relieved by his behavior, needing some emotional distance herself. Furthermore, she'd assumed he was as bone-tired as the rest of the cast and crew.

Now she wondered. Had Dion been trying to give her a silent message to keep away from him? Had his lovemaking been a momentary passionate urge?

And what did it all have to do with Sally and Jake?

Randi knew it was useless to conjecture, and she was unwilling to ask Dion questions. Rubbing her stomach, into which she had recently deposited a sizable breakfast, Randi felt empty again.

"We've done enough takes to make three movies," Chuck Brockman insisted. "All we need is a shot of the sorceress standing above the lake on that rock over there. We can do that tomorrow."

"I'd like an additional angle besides what we've got," Randi told him firmly, refusing to be intimidated by Chuck's experience, greater than hers in number of years.

"It's getting colder, and the light is going to change anytime now."

"We can manage for another hour."

"Whatever you say," Chuck said grudgingly, moving the camera into the position she'd requested.

If only she'd had more than one camera, Randi could

have spent less time on the scene. As it was, she felt the shots were crucial in the visual sequence of *Chrysalis,* and she wasn't about to sacrifice quality.

"I'm turning blue!" shouted Paul from where he was treading water in the center of the small, placid lake. "My goose bumps are turning into ostrich lumps!"

"Hang on. Only a few more shots," Randi yelled back. She nodded to Jake, who helped Nora out of the blanket in which she'd been wrapped for warmth. Scantily clad, the actress eased herself into the cold water and swam to Paul's side. Jocelyn and Dion watched from the shore.

Randi surreptitiously glanced at Dion. She had put aside her mixed feelings about him by ignoring his presence as much as possible that day.

"Move to the right," Randi told Nora. "We need a close-up."

Nora obligingly turned her face to the camera while Chuck rolled film. Everything went well until Nora's eyes bulged and she screamed.

"Yeek! Something bit me!" She began to thrash around in the water.

"Don't be afraid," advised Dion from the bank. "It's probably just a hungry trout. There's not much else in these waters."

"Cut!" yelled Randi.

"Looks like a scene from *Jaws,*" grumbled Chuck. "This will mean another take, I suppose?"

"There's nothing here, Nora." Paul comforted the actress by wrapping his arms around her. "It was just a fish —a small one."

"I know, but it startled me. Oooh! Tiny little rubbery lips nipping at my leg. How creepy!"

"Get ready to shoot again," said Randi impatiently.

"Get into position, Nora." She wanted to finish the water sequence today. Although she'd survived the fish incident, Nora's teeth were chattering.

As the cinematographer zoomed in for a close-up, Randi turned to Dion and Jocelyn. They'd been in the lake before, but she wanted to use them again from the newest angle.

"Get ready to go back in."

"We've got to freeze again?" asked Jocelyn. "I was very uncomfortable this morning."

"It *is* too cold, Randi." Dion seconded the notion. "Can't we do this tomorrow?"

"It won't be any warmer tomorrow. Besides, we're already set up for the shot," Randi explained. "I'm going to bring on the sorceress while you're in the water."

Dion sighed. "All right, here goes take number two hundred and eighty-five."

Randi ignored him, irritated that no one seemed to understand the importance of her request. After all, their discomfort would last only a few more minutes. Quickly she prepped Jake and Naomi, sending the actress to a position behind a rocky ledge jutting over the lake.

"Now. A wide angle with everyone in it," she told Chuck. Then, "Cut! Next shot! Spread out, Paul, Nora. I'd like a profile of Dion."

"Making sure you show Pretty Boy's best side?" the cinematographer questioned her snidely.

Registering the remark, Randi let it slide past her. She didn't want to spend the remaining few minutes of valuable shooting time on such nonsense. Not only that, but in her present mood, she was liable to lose her temper.

When Randi signaled for Nora and Paul to leave, the

couple did so gratefully. Lifting themselves onto the shore, they ran for the blankets.

"I want a soft focus on this," Randi told Chuck. "It will mirror the love scene that comes later."

Chuck grunted back at her, adding a filter to the lens.

Randi sized up the scene with a trained eye. It would be a beautiful shot. Just Shann and Lara in a mountain pool, their intermingled reflections blending with those of the surrounding rocks and firs.

"Look at him lovingly," she shouted to Jocelyn.

Peeking through the camera's eyepiece, she saw that the actress's expression looked like a grimace. Randi grew irritated. What was the matter? Had Jocelyn forgotten all her preparation?

"Jocelyn, think about how much he means to you! What you've been through together in the past few weeks," Randi called to her. "Shann's connected you to your inner passionate nature. You feel as one!"

Without permission, Randi's thoughts returned to her own love scene scant days ago, and her throat tightened. Would she learn to regret it? No! If she had to, she'd store the memory like some rare and precious footage. She refused to forget such an experience.

Randi peered through the eyepiece again. As she watched, Jocelyn turned so the back of her head was to the camera. Then the actress exchanged whispers with Dion.

"Jocelyn!" Randi shouted. "Turn around! You know better than that! Remember what we've been working on!"

"She's too cold to do anything," Dion yelled back angrily. "It's freezing in here!"

Randi bridled at his tone. "Two more minutes, please! We're almost done. Dion, fluff up your hair!"

"It's wet, in case you haven't noticed!"

Rolling her eyes, Randi willed herself to be patient. "Well, run a hand through it so it doesn't lie so flat against your head," she shouted, mentally adding, *empty as it may be.*

"Why don't we call in the makeup department, too, while we're about it!"

Dion's temper was going from bad to worse. Was she going to have a scene with him before this shoot was over? Randi wondered. She would if he planned to revert to his *Wrangler* days! Randi gritted her teeth. Jocelyn still looked decidedly unloving, but at least she was facing the camera.

"Okay. We're going to change things. Jocelyn, turn your head so we see a partial profile. Forget about an expression. Dion, *you* look loving!"

At least the actor was hers to command on camera, Randi thought with satisfaction. Despite a short bout of sneezing, Dion managed to assume the correct expression. Taking the shot, Randi called for the sorceress to appear on the rock above the pool.

"Just a few more minutes," she assured Dion and Jocelyn.

"That's what you said before!" complained Dion, sneezing again.

"Roll film!"

As Naomi appeared, arms raised, her blue robe flapping like wings in the wind, Randi directed the cameraman, "Now tilt down, Chuck, so we can see the lovers in the pool."

The cinematographer quickly complied. "That does

it," he said. "But I don't think you're going to like the big close-up at the end. Lover-boy's nose was running."

"It'll look natural!" Randi snapped, watching Dion help Jocelyn from the water.

The filming finished for the day, the entire group returned to camp. As Sam prepared the evening meal, Randi came out of her tent to search for Dion. She might as well face the unpleasantness immediately.

Whatever happened this morning in the clandestine meeting with Jake and Sally, she would try to put it out of her mind. If there was a traitor in the camp, Randi decided, she'd rather not know who it was, after all. At least she could attempt to clear up the friction with Dion. She found him sitting on the bedroll in his tent, blowing his nose into a tissue. When he looked up, she noticed that his nose was red and swollen, his usually bright blue eyes watery.

"Mind if I come in?" she asked cautiously.

"No."

She was put off by the short answer. Where was the tender lover of two days ago?

"Sorry, Foxy, I just don't feel well."

"Suffering again, I see," Randi said in an attempt at humor. Then, seriously, "I guess the exposure in the lake water didn't do you any good."

"I guess not."

"I'm sorry. I didn't realize you were coming down with a cold. Why didn't you say so?"

"Would it have mattered?"

She stared at him unbelievingly. "I'd like to get this project done the right way, but I'm not heartless."

"Sometimes you push people too hard."

"I don't ask anything of anyone I wouldn't do myself."

"Not everyone's as tough as you."

"I'm getting tired of hearing that word used to describe me."

Dion pulled a blanket around his shoulders. "And I'm just tired. Luckily I'm more secure than I was three years ago or you'd never hear the end of it."

"You were insecure then?"

"Why do you think I had such emotional outbursts during *Wrangler?* I was having a hard time, but you didn't offer to help me."

"You didn't seem to need any."

"I had my first dramatic role, and you kept pushing me."

"Why do we always come back to this?" Randi asked, feeling a burning sensation in her stomach.

"Because you were pushing Jocelyn this afternoon the same way you used to push me. You expected her to be able to emote in the middle of a frigid lake."

"I've prepped her and prepped her."

"And you're going to have to prep her some more. Nora and I have been working with her in our T-group, but it takes time to develop acting skills."

"All right." Randi sighed. "I suppose I was a little tense out there. We've all had long hours, and Chuck was giving me a hard time. I'll talk to Jocelyn."

Dion blew his nose again. "You were more than tense out there. You seemed angry. Why else make us stay in that icy pool for three hours?"

"It wasn't that long!" Randi's stomach twisted again. "And you were pretty testy yourself. If you hadn't tried to irritate me, things would have gone faster."

"I think we should quit discussing this now," Dion

said before erupting with a series of hacking coughs. "I feel so bad, I'm likely to say anything."

"I was just trying to do a good job," Randi muttered.

"As usual. Sometimes you're so hard to understand. I have to remind myself we're two different people with vastly different outlooks on accomplishing our goals. I just wish you'd quit trying to prove you're the perfect director." Randi's brow furrowed, and Dion said, "I can see I've hurt your feelings; I didn't mean to. I'd take you in my arms, but I feel too sick to cuddle you."

Randi didn't feel like being cuddled. She wanted to say something spiteful to Dion but carefully controlled herself. After all, he was sick, and she felt a little sorry for him.

"I'm going to the fire. Do you want some soup?"

"I think Nora's bringing me some." Dion seemed to want to say something, but he hesitated. Randi waited for him to continue. "You know, we'd better be careful about being seen together too much. There's a lot of gossip around this camp." Was this Dion's way of pushing her out of his life? Randi swallowed hard while he wound down. "In fact, maybe you'd better leave now before someone gets the wrong idea."

He was throwing her out of his tent! "I *was* leaving," she replied as she walked out without looking back. Her stomach churned, and her angry hurt was like a deep, open wound.

Throwing aside the tent flap, Randi wished the flimsy structure had a solid door to slam.

Striding to the cookfire, Randi grabbed a warm biscuit from a surprised Sam and savagely bit into it. Then she headed for the outer perimeters of the camp. Randi condemned Dion to the depths of the seven seas while circling a grove of pine trees several times. Searching for an appropriate name to call him, she decided Dion was more like a demon than a god.

Not having much experience with romantic complexities, Randi understood neither their tenuous relationship nor the nuances of dealing with Dion. Now if this were a movie she was directing, Randi was sure she'd have no difficulty in developing her characters or in understanding their motivations. Perhaps if she thought of her situation as a scene she was directing . . .

"En garde!" she cried suddenly, imagining a sword fight with the illusionary fiend. "Hmm. Running him through might give me some satisfaction, but our story has nothing to do with swords and sorcery. It's about human relationships. Let's see, how would I develop the characters?"

Thinking hard, Randi rubbed her chin and walked on. The heroine in her inner movie was easy to understand. She was wonderful, honest, pure of heart, someone deserving of love.

The hero/villain was more difficult to fathom. Was he an unthinking user who'd tasted the heroine's sweetest depths, then cast her aside? Or was his cruelty intentional? she asked herself with a melodramatic sweep of her arm. Did he harbor a secret desire for power over her, exercising it by playing with her body and emotions? Did he plan to tout his victory to others? What would he gain?

Randi frowned as she skirted a pile of rocks. Her ideas for character motivation were too simplistic, too black and white. She'd overlooked the obvious. Perhaps the hero and heroine were totally opposite personalities with overblown libidos, condemned to both repel and attract. What a setup for tragedy!

"What do you want from me, Dion?" Randi asked out loud, playing her heroine's role.

"Your body!" she replied, deepening her voice in the role of the hero.

"There's got to be something else!" cried Randi.

"How about love?" her imaginary Dion suggested.

"I don't believe it!"

Randi didn't know at which point she'd become aware of it, but she suddenly realized she had an audience. Whirling, she saw she was playing her scene to the tethered line of pack horses. Diablo seemed to be giving her a derisive eye.

"This is real interesting!" The wrangler in charge of the horses stepped out from the shadow of a tree. "I always wondered how you folks went about making them movies!"

"Uh . . ."

"You the director?"

"Yes."

"What a job! Acting out all them parts!"

"It's difficult," Randi admitted as though this were something she did every time she directed.

Smiling ironically at her own ridiculousness, Randi retreated to the camp. Dion was definitely affecting her.

Entering her tent and sinking down on the bedroll, she castigated herself for mixing work and romance. How foolish she'd been to answer Dion's lure! Shivering slightly, Randi wrapped her arms around herself, then remembered the feeling of being in his arms.

Had those few golden moments been worth it? Thinking of the water, the sky, the fires within, Randi decided they had. Then why were tears sliding down her cheeks?

As had been happening during the past few weeks, Randi felt overly emotional and confused. Why were real-life romances always so awful? Could she even call her relationship with Dion a romance?

"I just don't know," she exclaimed aloud, throwing the next day's script at her tent's yielding wall.

CHAPTER SEVEN

Having finished the segment of *Chrysalis* to be shot in the High Sierras, the cast and crew were on their way back to the studios at Sequoia Productions. Oblivious to the sways and jolts of the half-empty bus, Randi made copious notes to herself as she worked out a scene.

Sitting alone, her notebooks, script and papers spread over the long backseat, she tried to turn a deaf ear to the chattering and laughter up front, but it was with great difficulty that Randi stopped picking Dion's mellow tones out from the rest. Occasionally she would take a break from her work to look up. Invariably Dion's eyes would meet her own across the half-dozen vacant seats between them. Why wasn't he ignoring her, Randi wondered, just as he'd been doing for the past two weeks?

Actually that wasn't a fair assessment of the situation, she admitted to herself. Dion had treated her with the same friendly familiarity as he had before they'd come together at the waterfall—once he'd gotten over his cold, that is.

By that time Randi had convinced herself that she should think of Dion only as one of the actors rather than as a lover.

Annoyed with herself for beating a dead horse, Randi

forced herself to review the work she'd just done. Frowning, she wasn't surprised she couldn't get the love scene between Dion and Jocelyn right. She'd have to start over.

Engrossed in reworking the scene's blocking for the fifth time that morning, Randi was disconcerted when she realized Dion was standing over her. It was difficult to act distant and coolly professional when you could feel the blood rushing to your cheeks, Randi thought in disgust. Still, she attempted to put up a nonchalant front.

"Do you want something?"

"You," he said, arching an eyebrow provocatively. "Alone."

The line was familiar. "Oh, your libido acting up again? Don't worry," she said sarcastically, making a point of checking her watch, "in less than an hour you'll have your choice of women to take care of it."

Dion laughed, showing off his perfect white teeth. He made himself comfortable, sitting sideways in the seat directly in front of her, allowing his long legs to sprawl in the aisle.

"But I choose you, foxy lady."

"Sorry, I'm unavailable."

"Sure about that?"

"I have a lot of work to do."

"We've gone over that before."

"And my position hasn't changed."

"But something has."

"Yes, you have. You made it clear you weren't interested, but now you're trying to disturb me again. Why?"

Dion looked at her thoughtfully. "I had a feeling you took what I said the wrong way."

"When you told me we were two different people? Or when you threw me out of your tent?" she asked in a low

108

voice, anxiously looking past Dion, gratified their hushed conversation was going unnoticed.

"I did *not* throw you out of my tent. . . ."

"You didn't?" It was her turn to arch an eyebrow.

"Well, I didn't mean it that way. I thought it was best for you if we didn't flaunt our relationship. You were so upset about all the network's criticisms that I figured it wouldn't hurt to play it cool in front of the others."

"Then what are you doing sitting near me now? Someone might get the right idea."

"I changed my mind. I was wrong to give in to the pressure. To hell with gossip and the network's intimidation tactics."

Randi couldn't think of a clever retort. She sighed. "And have you changed your mind about our not being right for each other too?"

"I never said that."

"Not in those exact words, perhaps . . ."

"Randi, I've always thought we were right for each other. Not perfect, perhaps. At least not yet. But we can work on it."

"Speaking of perfect, I'm too much of a perfectionist for you, remember?"

"Maybe you need to change too."

"I'll never compromise my standards, Dion."

"No one asked you to. But you could think about modifying your approach. As long as the end results are the same, is that too much to ask?"

Randi tried to read through Dion's confident, serious exterior. Could she trust his words? Had he stayed away from her because he thought it was for her own good? Did he really think they were right for each other? Or did he have other motives for pursuing her? Randi wondered how she was supposed to tell if Dion's interest was genuine or an act.

He interrupted her thoughts. "So how about it?"

"How about what?"

"Spending some time together, just the two of us."

"When?"

"This weekend, starting tonight."

"You want to spend an entire weekend together?"

"You catch on fast. It'll be just you and me at my ranch."

The look of anticipation on his beautiful face made her defenses weaken. A sweet burning began deep inside her, just thinking about the possibilities. Oh, it was a tempting offer, in spite of the reservations Randi had about renewing their love affair. She could be badly hurt. But an entire weekend alone with Dion! Dare she take the risk?

"Say yes, Randi. It'll give us some time to get to know one another. We owe that to ourselves."

Trembling, she lost herself in his blue eyes. How could she not give it a chance?

"Yes," she said softly.

"Since we both have our cars at the studio lot, I'll follow you to your place and wait for you to pack."

"No. I'll take my own car to the ranch. Write down the directions and I'll meet you in a few hours."

"Always the independent woman, huh?"

"Always," Randi said with more conviction than she felt. She recognized that taking another chance on Dion Hayden was an impulsive gesture. Somehow, since the first time they'd made love, he'd always inspired her to impetuous acts. She wished she knew whether his influence was good or bad.

"Swimming? But I didn't bring a suit," Randi protested.

"Randi, it's almost dark and there's no one around for miles. I let my caretaker and housekeeper visit relatives for the weekend so we'd be alone. Who'll see?"

"You!"

Dion wiggled his eyebrows. "Right!"

Randi looked at the remainder of the gigantic garden sandwich he'd made her—only one tiny bite—and wished she hadn't eaten it and a fruit salad with such unbridled enthusiasm. Swimming with a man who was in such perfect condition, she'd have felt self-conscious *with* a suit, but naked and stuffed? Ouch.

"I've never been into water sports," she said weakly.

"I'm not interested in athletics. Swimming at night is so peaceful. Imagine floating on your back, watching the stars."

Randi recognized the longing in Dion's expression. It had nothing to do with swimming. Nervously she realized he wanted her as much as she did him. But how were they supposed to get to know one another better if all they did was make love? Maybe swimming would keep things on an even keel a little while longer.

"All right."

"Good," Dion said, tenderly patting her mouth with a napkin, then leading her out onto the redwood deck.

Dion's ranch was a quiet hideaway north of Los Angeles. Built on a small ridge, the trilevel house of rough-hewn cedar afforded them a spectacular view from every direction. Pastureland mixed with coyote country. Scrub, sagebrush and scattered evergreens dotted the landscape. Randi knew hills rolled out into mountains, although they now faded into the distance as darkness settled. The only buildings in their line of vision were the barn in the pasture and the cottage, which normally housed Dion's caretaker and housekeeper.

"I do love your privacy. It makes me feel like we're in a world of our own."

"That was the idea." Dion squeezed Randi's hand and, as if sensing her shyness about swimming in the nude, said, "I meant to bring out some wine. Why don't you go ahead? By the time you get undressed and slip into the pool, I'll be back with a bottle and two glasses."

"It's a deal."

All three levels of the main house opened onto the redwood deck. It eventually gave way to sand-colored granite surrounding the free-form pool with its tiny waterfall. Granite steps led up to the similarly designed hot tub on the same level as the master bedroom. And the landscaping—bushes, cacti, flowers and imported palm trees—pulled everything together as if the setting were natural rather than man-made.

Randi quickly slipped out of her rust gauze pants and shirt and into the pool. How heavenly! she thought, floating on her back and enjoying her view of the stars.

"Good thing I went back. I forgot the towels too," Dion said. Randi righted herself and began to tread water as he stepped onto the granite terrace and put the towels, the wine cooler and the glasses onto a rattan table. "It might be a little chilly when we get out."

Watching him strip slowly—purposefully provocatively, she was sure—Randi didn't think she would be anything but hot while she was with him that night. When he slid off his shirt, her eyes eagerly traveled over his firm torso, across his broad shoulders, down his smoothly muscled chest with its light fur of golden curls, to his narrow waist.

Randi plunged backward, wetting her head and face, trying to ease the flame already building within her. Hurry, she thought, her eagerness to keep things on an even keel laid to rest for the moment. But Dion was in no hurry to relieve her building frustration. After unfastening his belt and unzipping his pants, he lazily reached for the wine bottle and poured two glasses, then walked to the edge of the pool.

"Come get your wine," he said, crouching on his haunches.

Randi made her way to the edge of the pool, where the water was barely deep enough to cover her nipples. Hard and aching, they were the center of Dion's attention. He watched closely as her breasts gently bobbed along the surface of the water. If his expression was any indication, steam would rise out of the cool water once he joined her in the pool.

As she took the glass, Randi saw the golden hair starting just below his waist. Her eyes widened when she realized curls weren't all that was exposed by the open zipper. He wasn't wearing any underwear.

Dion touched the side of her head and stroked the wet waves of her russet hair.

"To getting to know one another better," he said as he raised his wineglass.

They clinked glasses and sipped. Dion set down his glass and stood, then stripped off his pants. He was ready for her, Randi realized, her pulse quickening in expectation. But when he slid into the water, he picked up his glass and relaxed against the edge of the pool.

"What do you think of this wine?"

113

"What?"

"The wine. A friend of mine is the vintner. Do you like it?"

"I . . . uh . . ." She'd been so wrapped up in her burgeoning desire for Dion, Randi hadn't really tasted it. She took a small sip and rolled it in her mouth. "Nice. Very nice."

"You like wines that aren't totally dry, then."

"Uh, yes."

Confused, Randi avoided his eyes and drank. Why were they talking about wines when she wanted nothing more than to feel Dion deep inside her?

"Hey, not so fast." Taking the glass from her hand, Dion set it on the edge of the pool along with his own. "I'm not trying to get you drunk."

Now, she thought. He's going to make love to me now. Randi knew her lips were curving in a silly little grin. When Dion turned back to her, he grinned too. Cupping her cheeks with both hands, he kissed her softly.

"You know what I really want to do?" he murmured, his lips finding her ear.

"Hm-m-m?" she purred, rubbing herself against him.

"Swim. C'mon."

Randi was too surprised to protest. Dion dragged her into deep water, challenging her to a race. Reluctant at first, Randi soon relaxed. They raced to the waterfall and let it pour over them as they kissed. Then Dion lured her from the edge so he could dunk her. Sputtering as she came up for air, Randi sought revenge.

They played in the water for almost an hour. Then Dion insisted they try the hot tub. Wrapped in the large towels, carrying full wineglasses, they quickly made their way up the granite stairs. Randi wondered what it would be like to make love in a hot tub, but she didn't find out. Dion was more interested in talking.

He must have noted the confusion that gradually settled on her features, because he stopped in the middle of a sentence and said, "Randi, do you mind terribly if we don't make love tonight?"

"I . . . is something wrong?"

Dion's lips parted in a beautiful smile. "No. Everything is right, and I want to keep it that way. I was serious about wanting us to know one another better. If we make love now, I doubt we'll have time to do anything else this weekend. Besides, I don't want you to think I'm only satisfying my libido."

A smile began deep inside Randi and blossomed out to her lips. "How about a kiss?"

"Your wish is my command."

The kiss was warm and tender, as satisfying as Dion's more passionate embraces. It had to be difficult for him to stop with a kiss, for Randi noted he was ready for much more. As they talked for hours, she realized she'd never felt happier.

Once in a state of euphoria, she found it hard to settle down. Even by low lamplight, Dion's bedroom reflected the pale tones of bleached woodwork and beams overhead. The ecru carpeting, caramel leather chaise cushions and raw silk pillows and shams complemented his golden aura.

Randi knew she'd be awake all night, especially since Dion insisted she sleep there instead of in the guest bedroom so he could hold her in his arms, but she slept better than she had since beginning work on *Chrysalis*.

At dawn he served her breakfast in bed, then insisted they ride so he could show her his property. When she balked at getting on a horse again, Dion said he planned to teach her to be as comfortable mounted as on foot. After a two-hour ride, when Randi grumbled that he'd have to teach her backside as well, he whisked her off to the hot tub.

They lunched, then swam, and after a joint bath in the master bedroom's sunken tub, which was raised high and surrounded with windows for a spectacular view of the countryside, they napped. It was dusk when Dion woke her with a kiss.

"Get up, sleepyhead. I'm ready to start dinner."

"More food? Dion, I won't fit into any of my clothes!"

"Then we'll buy you more. I have a thing for fleshy women," he mumbled, nuzzling her neck. "It's the Greek in me."

Smiling, Randi said, "I didn't know you were Greek."

"Part. I have a Greek grandfather. Where do you think I got a name like Dionysus? My heritage hasn't hurt my culinary skills either. Now come on!"

Randi rose but headed for the bathroom. "I have to powder my nose. Meet you in the kitchen."

By the time she had freshened up and slipped into a beige caftan that bared one shoulder, Dion was making clattering noises and singing loudly to himself.

Affectionately Randi watched him work from the doorway. He seemed as confident in the dramatic cedar-faced kitchen as he was everywhere else, mixing things without using a cookbook, adding spices without measuring them. Dion cooked as he lived, Randi thought, spontaneously and free-flowing.

Finally he noticed her. "Trying to steal my recipe?"

"Uh-uh. To steal a kiss." Dion held out his arms in

116

invitation, and Randi attacked him. "M-m-m. Garlic. Delicious."

After dinner, they shared another bottle of wine in the main living area. Dion made himself comfortable on the plush cotton-covered sofa, while Randi curled up next to him. Again, they talked, their conversation eventually shifting to their careers.

"While I was still working on my master's degree, I had very definite goals," Randi said. "My dream was to be a top-notch film director. Accordingly, I made a schedule of where I should be in my career by when, never realizing how truly naive I was. I believed if I did my job well, I would be rewarded."

Dion squirmed. "Life doesn't always work that way."

"Especially not in Hollywood," Randi agreed. "That's why I got tough, I guess. My schedule had to be adjusted, but my goals stayed the same."

"Must you plan your happiness, Randi? Why can't you live for now? Enjoy today. Take things as they come."

Randi frowned. She'd been trying to forget the things that might make a relationship between them impossible, but with that comment, they came back to her clearly. Enjoy today. Was that how he saw his time with her? To be enjoyed, then forgotten?

"I won't give up my dream."

"Don't give it up, but don't let ambition destroy your life." There was a disturbing quality to his tone. Randi waited. A painful expression crossed Dion's face as he explained. "I had a very ambitious friend named Kent. He was a damn fine actor, not just a glitzy glamour boy."

"I take it he didn't succeed."

"Hell, he's dead!"

A lump formed in Randi's throat when she saw the

pain in Dion's eyes. "Want to talk about it?" For a moment she thought he'd refuse, but he obviously needed her to know.

"We were best friends. In college Kent majored in drama. I majored in having a good time. He asked me to audition with him for a TV sitcom because he needed my support, only I got the part. The director took one look and said, 'That's my boy!' "

"Just like that?"

"Uh-huh. I quit school and lived it up, blowing money like it was going out of style. I was too wrapped up in my own ego to see what was happening to Kent. Desperation's a sad thing. Walk-on parts, that was all he ever got, while I was a star. Then one day I woke up scared. The series was canceled. What was I going to do? I didn't know how to do anything else, but I didn't have the talent to compete with real actors. All I'd ever done was play me. I don't know how my agent got me in *Wrangler*, but that movie was it for me. I *had* to be good."

"And I thought all you cared about was making money the easy way. I thought that was why you were . . . so difficult."

"I was bad-tempered because *I* was desperate then. Wouldn't you be if you were twenty-six and didn't know what you were going to do with the rest of your life? No," Dion said quietly, "Randi St. Martin always knew what she was capable of."

"But I didn't make it any easier for you."

"That's not totally true. I respected you, so when I knew you were interested in me, it made me feel good about myself. And when we made love, I felt even better. You're so real, so solid. I should have called. Let me tell you why I never did."

118

"It's in the past. You don't have to."

"I need to. My role in *Wrangler* got me another part, and I managed to pull strings for Kent. It was only a minor role, but it was a good one." Dion's face took on a new tenseness as he went on. "He got himself fired for refusing to do a scene—he just wouldn't compromise himself—then called me to complain about the director. Instead of listening, I told him to stop feeling sorry for himself and get his act together. See, *I* wasn't desperate anymore."

The muscles of his jaw tightened. Randi slipped her hand to his leg, trying to communicate her support. "And that's when he killed himself?" she asked, already knowing the answer.

Dion nodded. "It made me feel like the lowest of worms. If only I had taken the time to listen and to try to help."

"It wasn't your fault. He made his own choice."

"Maybe, but I didn't do anything to stop it from happening. I wasn't there when my best friend needed me. I wanted to call you and talk about it, Randi, but I couldn't. I lost the little respect I had for myself and thought you'd blame me. You were the model of integrity, the epitome of a Hollywood professional." Dion cupped her face and rubbed her cheek with his thumb. "Now I know I underestimated you."

Feeling a bit guilty herself, Randi couldn't say a word. Would she have understood? Given the awful way she had been torn in her feelings about Dion at that time, she might have worsened his pain.

"I told you I changed," Dion went on. "I was so depressed I couldn't work. With professional help, I recognized the important things in life. Fame and success are great as long as they don't prevent you from having friends . . . a close relationship with your family . . . someone to love."

Randi knew her eyes widened. Dion was looking at her so tenderly. *Someone to love.* Did he mean her? What was he trying to tell her?

Dion shook his head. "I was too young and shallow to be any good for you three years ago. I loved you then but didn't know how to tell you. Can you accept my love now?"

Dion didn't wait for her to answer but leaned over and kissed her gently.

Any leftover reservations she might have had about continuing their relationship flew away like caged birds suddenly freed. Randi fully gave herself to the feelings aroused by the kiss. Gently she placed her palms on either side of Dion's face and sent her eager tongue exploring. His response was a muted groan.

Intensely involved, she didn't realize he'd slid off the sofa and was kneeling before her until he placed an arm beneath her knees.

"I want to lie beside you, Randi. It's time."

Standing, he lifted her from the chair and started up the cedar stairs.

"You don't have to carry me," Randi protested softly.

"I know. But I'm afraid to let you throw me over *your* shoulder."

Randi laughed. "I may be tough, but I don't lift weights."

"Oh, I see. Now you're accusing me of being dead weight." Dion winked playfully, assuring Randi that he bore no grudges.

Entering the open doors of the master bedroom, he

laid her on the bed's cotton comforter. In the light from the ecru-shaded lamp, he looked more desirable than ever.

"You're so beautiful, Foxy. And part of your beauty is you don't even know it."

Taking the hem of her long caftan, he began to strip her of the garment. She helped by lifting her hips, then her shoulders. In seconds she lay naked against the cool cotton. Dion took a deep breath. With gestures that made Randi tremble, he ran his hands lightly over her smooth body.

"Look at yourself!" Dion demanded. "How can you possibly think you need to starve yourself constantly?"

Glancing down, Randi watched Dion's hand encircle the ripe globe of one breast. His other hand traced the curve of her rounded belly, then slid over the lush flesh of her hip.

"You're voluptuous," he told her. "As curvaceous as the earth itself. And I'm a man who appreciates earthiness." Capturing a blush-colored nipple between two fingers, he made Randi catch her breath. "Here's the tip of a mountain," he said as he teased her breast. "Down lower is the fertile plain. . . . Your body holds a thousand treasures for me."

Raising her head slightly, Randi glanced down at her body and noticed how her flesh took on a rosy luminosity in the flattering lamplight. Seeing herself through Dion's poetic eyes, Randi thought perhaps she *was* beautiful. Had her thighs always looked so delightfully curved?

Dion nuzzled Randi's shoulder while he unzipped his jeans. Turning to help him, she pulled the denim over his slim hips. She caressed his turgid flesh, then gave him an impetuous, intimate kiss. Next she drew her tongue along his hard length, teasing him with tiny nips until Dion shuddered.

With a fluid movement Dion stretched out on the bed, drawing Randi tightly against him. She could feel his swollen warmth touching the tender skin of her inner thighs. Moving her hips provocatively, she invited him to enter her.

But Dion wasn't to be hurried. His mouth near hers, he whispered, "I want to taste your treasures first."

Starting with her lips, he placed fiery kisses on her face and throat. Soon, drawing one turgid nipple into his mouth, then the other, he sipped at her breasts. His gentle, coaxing mouth drew forth Randi's deepest passion. Her nipples felt like burgeoning buds ready to burst into exotic bloom. She almost exploded when his fingers found the hot desire between her thighs.

Dion allowed his lips to trace the path his hand had taken. With sweet, spiraling intensity, Randi let him lead her. His mouth was tender, evocative. Seeing colors surge behind her eyelids, she cried out.

But the journey had only started. Dion positioned himself over her and gained entrance to the maze of her delight. Gently, then faster, he rocked her in the age-old dance of life. Randi tilted her hips to meet him as Dion searched her deepest passageways. Following dark, labyrinthine paths, she joined the quest, wondering what they would find at the end.

There seemed to be a light somewhere. Randi was ecstatic as she and Dion moved as one. Its brilliance grew stronger, brighter . . . she could almost see the source . . . it was piercing, golden like a pulsing star. But upon seeing it, Randi caught her breath and fell, trembling and

122

tumbling. The light shattered into a thousand shining fragments as Randi cried out again.

Dion had been with her. Satiated now, he rested against her, his breathing slowly returning to normal.

"I love you," he whispered, laying his head on her breast.

Later, as a clean wind fluttered the curtains, Randi lay wide-eyed in the dark bedroom, remembering the words to which she'd had no response. Dion slept soundly at her side. Physically she felt peaceful and whole, but her anxious mind would not let her rest.

Dreamlike images drifted across her consciousness, mystery caves and ancient footsteps leading into the winding labyrinth. What was the secret she had seen so clearly?

Had Dion finally revealed his true self to her? Had he verbalized his innermost feelings? Did unspoken mysteries lurk in her own depths? Was she ready to face the possibility that she might love him in return?

Revelations could be dangerous if Randi wasn't ready to face the truth.

"He said he loved me," she whispered aloud.

Turning her face against the comforting pillow of Dion's curls, Randi remembered something she'd read: All paths were the same and they all went somewhere; if you have a choice, follow the path with the heart in it.

Should she take that advice? Randi wasn't sure.

CHAPTER EIGHT

Standing perplexed in her condo's small kitchen, Randi watched two cloves of garlic bounce whole and untouched off the blades of her food processor.

"How on earth do you puree the stuff?" Obviously *this* wasn't the way.

As she stopped the machine with one hand, Randi rummaged across the crowded countertop with the other. Her French gourmet cookbook had to be nearby. Randi had been reading it just before she'd laid out the ingredients and all the utensils she owned to make crevettes à la Grecque—Greek-style shrimp.

The recipe had appeared deceptively simple, making Randi think she could exercise what basic culinary skills she possessed to make a special dinner for Dion. Now she wondered if "simple gourmet" was too difficult for her.

"Ah!" She found the book hiding beneath a cutting board. Before flipping it open, she glanced at the television and video recorder pulled up on a stand near the kitchen door. She'd rented a videotape of one of Dion's old movies, hoping to watch it as she prepared dinner. But the way things were going, she would be lucky to see much of the film.

"Run!" Dion's voice cried as a close-up of his face filled the screen. *"They're coming after us!"*

A chase scene ensued. As Randi watched, she realized why the thriller had been so popular the year before. *Distant Lightning* was fast-paced, and Dion had handled the lead role well. It seemed he'd been an accomplished actor for some time. Randi thought about renting his other movies and catching up on them—if she ever managed to see this one all the way through!

Frowning, she forced herself to read the recipe again, but the instructions were no more clear than the first time. "Forget it!" she muttered, tossing the paperback aside. Improvising as she went, she hoped this meal for Dion would be edible.

They'd had a wonderful time at his ranch the preceding weekend. Her lips curved into a slow smile as a fluttering warmth spread throughout her body. She and Dion had enjoyed more than the sensuality of food.

Randi tightened the apron around her waist. Would Dion like the new outfit underneath? The two-piece hostess dress was cream cotton printed with exotic melon and blue flowers. Its sarong skirt was slit to above her thigh, and the low-cut top left her midriff bare. The garment was definitely a departure from her usual style.

Dion will approve, she decided. He seemed to appreciate every curve of her rounded body. Randi had never felt so special around any man. Excitement starting to lick at her like small flames, she steered her thoughts to the problem at hand, realizing she had less than an hour to finish. She'd chop the garlic after she started the rice.

Brushing a dark lock from her forehead, Randi glanced back at the television. Dion and a woman detective, his romantic interest in the movie, were embracing on the small screen.

"We have to live for the moment," Dion told the woman. *"There may not be another chance. The most important thing in life is having someone to love."*

Randi raised her eyebrows. The words sounded familiar. As she watched Dion kiss his on-screen lover, a hissing sound came from the stove. The rice was boiling over! Quickly she turned the heat down.

When her attention returned to the videotape, Dion and the detective were in bed. He was bare to the waist. Randi wondered jealously if he wore anything beneath the sheet. How would she get used to having a relationship with a man who acted in filmed love scenes?

Concentrating carefully on her cooking, Randi nearly jumped out of her skin when the doorbell rang. He was early! Throwing aside the apron, she ran for the entryway, almost tripping over the television cord.

"Damn!" Randi reached to turn off the set.

Subliminally she noted Dion holding his lover and whispering, *"We're poetry together."*

Randi snapped off and unplugged both television and recorder just as the doorbell's harsh sound reverberated through the apartment again. Then she ran to the door and tried to open it with a studied casualness, posing to show off her new outfit.

"I thought I was in the wrong part of Pasadena . . . Foxy!" Dion's eyes sparkled wickedly as he slid his hands around Randi's bare waist. "Are you the first course or the dessert?"

"Both!" Randi nestled against his hard body, offering her mouth for a kiss.

126

As his lips touched hers, Randi nibbled at them. "Hungry too?" he murmured.

Randi reluctantly pulled away. "Let's eat the food first. I went to a lot of trouble preparing it."

"If you insist," he teased. "May I set the table?"

"How about putting the wine on ice?"

"Wine? Oh, no!" Dion slapped his forehead. "I got so involved in my Technique session, I forgot it! I'll have to go buy some."

"Don't bother. I've got some rosé we can drink."

"But I promised to bring a dry white wine. French, right?"

"It's not that important."

"Are you sure?"

To convince him, Randi kissed Dion thoroughly. "Now, sit down," she insisted. "I'm going to stuff your gorgeous face."

During dinner Randi realized why Dion had forgotten the wine. Between compliments on her food and her appearance, he raved on and on about the class he'd just attended in Los Angeles. Randi heard about "experiencing characters" while they ate their salad and "flowing with dialogue" during the main course. By dessert and coffee, Dion was expounding on the constructive social features of studying the Technique.

"The members of the group are like friends; we support each other. Today we helped a guy celebrate his divorce."

"Celebrate his divorce?"

Noticing the slight frown on Randi's face, Dion hastened to explain. "It wasn't a happy event, but we wanted to help the man have a positive attitude. Sometimes you have to accept things the way they are."

"Uh-huh. Live for the moment." Randi was reminded of the Hollywood style of quick marriages and quicker divorces, with a lot of playing around in between.

"He didn't want a divorce, but it was the best thing for him under the circumstances."

"Oh."

Taking a bite of pears poached in wine sauce, Dion went on. "You'll have to excuse my overly enthusiastic babble, Foxy. After I attend a T-group, I'm really up. If it bothers you, tell me."

"I want to hear about what's important to you." Randi deliberated a moment, staring at the fresh flowers she'd arranged earlier as a centerpiece. "I'm curious, though. You said this was a reconnection session. I thought you'd just taken a series of classes. How long does the Technique last?"

"T-groups last as long as we want to go. And pay, of course."

"They sound like ongoing therapy groups."

"In a way they sometimes are. Mainly we learn state-of-the-art acting methods. And we make friends. There's always somebody around from a previous session. It's like belonging to a private professional club."

Randi didn't know why, but something about the Technique was beginning to bother her. Was it because Dion constantly used the pronoun *we* instead of *I* in referring to it? Being extremely independent, Randi had always refused to identify with a group.

"If you're curious," Dion said, "I can get you into an introductory class. Directors can learn from a method approach too."

"Um. I'm going to be busy checking on the special effects for *Chrysalis* this week."

128

"You don't have to do it right away."

"After that you know we're heading for location in the Mojave Desert."

"You're not interested in the Technique, are you?"

"I just don't think it's my type of thing."

Dion grinned, gazing at her with eyes that were electrifying in their blue intensity. "That's okay—as long as I am!" Moving his chair back from the table, he stood and held out his hand. "Come on, Foxy. Why don't you show me the rest of your condo? I want to know everything about you."

Randi allowed him to lead her into the living room, his arm pressing her close against his side. Her pulse quickened as she thought of the pleasure the night would bring.

"This isn't a showplace like your house. It's basically a place to sleep and read when I'm not on location." Suddenly Randi wished she'd hung more prints on the bare stucco walls or purchased something more stylish than the plain beige couch occupying one end of the room. She never seemed to have enough time to decorate. Gesturing toward the sliding glass doors leading to a small deck, she said, "I don't have a garden, but there's a nice view of the mountains in daylight."

"You've got interesting books." Dion ran his free hand over the spines of a shelfful.

"Everything you'd want to know about film and television."

"And what's this?" He touched the spires of a tiny pink castle sitting on her desk. "A paperweight?" Loosening his hold on her, Dion bent to examine it.

"A gift from . . . an old friend. It was hand-carved in

129

Germany." Randi still didn't think the time was right to reveal her relationship with Olga.

"You've got a lot of neat things in here." Dion stood back and tilted his head to look at the topmost shelves of a bookcase. "A sailboat and a rocket ship. Hm . . . and a couple of plastic robots."

"I have a collection of miniatures—dwellings, vehicles, animals, creatures and people—fantasy and otherwise."

Dion raised his eyebrows with interest as he inspected her shelves. "You must have started as a kid."

"Some are models from commercials I've directed, but others are toys I played with as a child," she admitted.

"That's great! I appreciate an adult who can still play."

Played, in the past tense. Actually I didn't play with them in the usual sense even then." At Dion's curious look, she explained. "I used to imagine scenes and direct them, using my toys as props and characters."

"Ah, you created your own world."

"I guess. I spent a lot of time alone, since I'm an only child and both my parents worked. They treated me like a small grown-up when I was with them. But usually they left me with housekeepers or at boarding schools, so I tended to make up quiet games in my head. My best friend was my godmother, who gave me many of these as gifts. She was rather eccentric and liked to collect miniatures herself."

"It sounds like you had a creative childhood, Foxy, but didn't you miss your parents?"

"My parents were so busy being successful in the movie industry, they didn't have time to worry about me."

"That's terrible!"

"They loved me," Randi said defensively. "But they

130

got caught up in their profession. My parents are a script-writing team. Unfortunately, they were never choosy about their employers or the quality of scripts they were hired to write. They thought they couldn't afford to be particular." She sighed. "Their last collaboration was the teen slasher movie that's showing now—*Birthday Party Massacre.*"

Dion tried to hide a smile behind his hand. "No wonder you're so big on values and quality, Foxy."

"I learned what *not* to do from my parents."

Randi didn't tell Dion about the industry horror stories her father had related as she grew up, or the fact that neither of her parents had wanted her to work in movies. It was from them she'd gotten her doubts and fear that tinsel often lay under the showy gold of Hollywood. Both her parents disliked actors. What would they think if they knew she and Dion were lovers? she wondered.

"You've got more of a background in movie-making than I do," Dion admitted. "Of course, I have more of a background in being a regular kid. I grew up playing rough and tumble with two brothers, three sisters and several dogs. My mother was noisy and loving, my father rough but affectionate. I forget how many aunts, uncles and cousins I have." He rubbed his chin. "Everybody butted into everybody else's business and tried to tell them what to do. With such intervention it's a wonder I ever felt grown up. My later experiences probably contributed to that."

He looked thoughtful. Randi knew he was thinking of his friend who had died and of his own mistakes.

She slipped her hand into his warm one, interlacing their fingers. "That's enough about backgrounds. Let's change the subject."

Dion grinned at her, the serious look disappearing from his face. "Good idea." He picked up a plastic, saucer-shaped spaceship two feet in diameter. "Isn't this the *Millennium Falcon* from *Star Wars?*"

"Right."

"Hm-m. I don't think you used *this* in a commercial, and you can't have owned it as a child."

"All right, so I bought it a few years ago. It's a good-luck piece. I liked *Star Wars* and respect George Lucas. He was a rebel, but he made it big while keeping his integrity. I'd like to be able to do the same. Make it big *my* way, values intact."

"I think you will." With that quiet assertion Dion raised the ship to eye level and began to move it back and forth, imitating the sounds of space flight. Stopping to glance around the room, Dion said, "We need a captain. There he is!" Picking up a small plastic man with movable arms and legs, he popped the figure through the *Falcon*'s hatch door. "Another gift from Olga?"

"Yes it is." Then she realized what he'd asked. "How did you know?"

"Maybe it was the way she spoke of you with such affection when I saw her about doing Shann. In addition, Olga's definitely eccentric and she collects miniatures."

"Don't tell anyone. It would be bad for the miniseries."

"I know more of your secrets," he whispered conspiratorially. "But you can buy my silence."

She could imagine the payment he expected.

Dion swept the ship around the room again. "Click, click, click," he said, imitating the crackling of a communications system. "This is Captain Farstar. Can anyone read me? I need a woman real bad." He circled Randi, flying the *Falcon* around her waist and hips. "Whew! I just orbited a heavenly body!"

Randi laughed. His zany behavior was infectious. "What's your mission, Captain Farstar?"

"I'm searching for someone to love me! Isn't there a woman somewhere in this universe who can appreciate my tight-fitting uniform?"

He had such a forlorn expression, Randi couldn't help herself. "Okay. You asked for it. Now I'm going to ravish you! Take off that uniform!"

"Please be gentle!" Dion pleaded, running his hands beneath Randi's long skirt and up her bare legs.

Legs? Looking down, Randi saw Dion lying on his back next to her feet. He'd put the spaceship aside.

She pounced on him, laughing. Dion laughed, too, pulling her over him, kissing the soft flesh of her breasts where the tops rounded over her low-cut bodice.

"M-m-m-m," Dion murmured. "Captain Farstar's been caught by a winged woman. Are we going to explore the universe together? Plan to take me on a ride to the stars?"

Randi laughed as she squirmed against him. *She* was the one who was caught! Placing her hands on either side of Dion's chest, she managed to raise her upper torso. While one of his strong arms kept her lower body pinned, he unfastened the dress top, freeing her full breasts.

Dion's eyes sparkled admiringly. "The stars are getting closer, and are they beautiful!"

As she gazed into his rapt face, Randi became strongly aroused by his usually clear blue eyes, which were now clouded with passion, and by his sensual lips, which curved into an anticipatory grin. Tugging his shirt up over his chest, she gently stroked him with her breasts.

He gasped as her firm nipples brushed the tips of his smaller ones.

As if realizing that Randi intended to accept his erotic invitation, Dion loosened his hold. She sat up on her knees, straddling him, then untied the knot of her sarong. Throwing the skirt aside, she slowly undulated her hips. Through the layers of fabric of his chino pants and her lacy briefs, she could feel his hard arousal.

Dion ran exploring fingers along the tender skin of her inner thigh, sending them to find the secrets hidden by her undergarment's lace edge.

Randi almost cried out at his intimate touch.

"How about exploring *inner* space?" she proposed breathlessly.

"After you, my fearless leader."

Randi began by removing the rest of their clothing. Then, as she positioned herself over him, she leaned forward to meet Dion's lips in a searching kiss. Their breath melding, their tongues caressing, she shaped her pliant flesh against his harder outline.

"Your loyal follower is about to mutiny," Dion groaned.

Taking over the lead, he completed their union by raising her willing hips and maneuvering them so Randi slid down his smooth length. She caught her breath at the thrill of sensation brought by the action. Breaking the spell of the kiss, Dion forced her erotic focus to a new, deeper area of pleasure.

"I love you, Randi." He touched her face so she would look at him. "And I truly want us to be together."

"I love you too, Dion."

Had she finally said it? Randi took no time for reflection, yet she felt lighter, her spirit uplifted. Her desire sweeping her to intense, sweet heights, Randi could imagine she was soaring into the skies.

Why had she been so afraid to face Dion and tell him of her feelings? Randi wondered. Her admission of love had blessed her with a rare sense of freedom. Lying in bed, cradled against Dion's chest, she savored the evening behind them and smiled into the darkness.

Dion was like no man she'd ever known—a golden, warmhearted lover. How much happiness she'd felt when he arrived at her door that day! Time spent with Dion always seemed to bring revelations to her, uncoverings of deep, hidden emotion. Finally Randi had discovered the gift of love.

She smiled as she thought of Captain Farstar's line: "Plan to take me on a ride to the stars?" Then, later, Dion had said, "I truly want us to be together." Had he been hinting at a more permanent relationship? Randi hoped so.

Their lovemaking on the living room rug had been tender and erotic. Remembering the heights of passion to which they'd soared together, Randi snuggled contentedly next to her sleeping lover's body, curling one foot inside his instep.

Had there been even one part of the evening that hadn't been perfect?

Randi had been annoyed with Dion's talk of the Technique. But he'd been able to use the method to become an accomplished actor. She respected his abilities, which he'd learned long ago, judging by the movie she'd rented. Before she returned it Randi would make an effort to watch the rest of the videotape. Thinking about how well he'd been suited to the role, one of his lines echoed through her mind.

"We're poetry together."

The words sounded vaguely familiar. Frowning, Randi was sure she remembered Dion using similar words to her. Was it at Olga's house? Mentally shrugging, she decided it must be a coincidence.

Enough thinking! Once again Randi was keeping herself awake. Rearranging her body, she slipped an arm across Dion's chest. He stirred without waking and made sleep sounds that engulfed Randi with warmth.

Finally closing her eyes, her thoughts drifted back to their playful lovemaking, which had definitely stirred her imagination. Randi wondered what it would be like to coast on the wind and dreamed of flying again with Dion.

CHAPTER NINE

"Ye gods! I'm really flying!" Randi shrieked and giggled simultaneously as she rose above the grayed head of her special effects director. The exhilarating sensation of momentary weightlessness set the pit of her stomach tumbling. "What am I supposed to do now?"

"Depends," Robb Ochs said, his attitude typically casual. "You can spread your wings and flap 'em or take it easy and float."

"How about if I want to be Superman?"

Aggressively Randi threw her body forward and stuck out one fist like the movie character, but she didn't stop level, as she had expected. She took a nosedive instead.

"Best be careful," Robb warned as she shrieked again. "That gag can be dangerous. What would Emily and Frank think if you got hurt?"

"They'd say their daughter was old enough to know better than to try a fool stunt." An old friend of her parents, Robb had fascinated Randi with his bag of mechanical tricks since her childhood. Wire work was one of his specialties. "Move me along the track, would you? I want to understand what Naomi will experience during her scene."

"Sure thing, Ariadne." Long ago Randi had given up

trying to dissuade Robb from using her proper name. Privilege came with age, he'd insisted. "Stay relaxed, but don't go flip-floppin' around none."

What had gotten into her? Randi wondered as she floated forward and *ooh*ed with delight.

The special shade of the blue screen behind her allowed the execution of a perfect motion effect. Using this particular special effect, the sorceress in *Chrysalis* would seem to fly, with the mountain scenery of the High Sierra behind her. The sequence was sure to be spectacular.

After a conference with the entire special effects staff, Randi hadn't been able to resist trying out the flying mechanism herself. Eagerly she'd climbed into the hip harness of molded fiber glass, doubtfully eyeing the steel piano wires running from her hips to a spreader above. Robb had assured her the slender wires would hold double her weight.

"Enough?" he asked as she completed a circle.

Laughing, Randi begged, "Please, one more time."

"You'd think you were a kid," Robb grumbled, but he didn't stop the machinery.

A kid. That was exactly what she felt like. Dion's influence was still with her from the other night, she guessed. This was the first time Randi had tried out one of her own special effects personally, though she'd been using them in commercials for years.

"I'd love to be able to fly through life like this!"

"If I didn't know how sensible you were, Ariadne, I'd think you were into that Technique thing."

"Why do you say that?" she asked breathlessly from above.

"Because people who are in it are flaky."

Randi laughed. "Thanks for the compliment, Robb. You can let me down now."

"No offense. Actin' a little strange, aren't you?" Robb adjusted the controls so that she stopped within several feet of him. He clucked, "Tch-tch. Wantin' to fly through life. Too many immature kids get their lives all tangled up over that Technique crap."

"Sounds personal," Randi said as her feet touched solid earth and her exhilaration died a reluctant death.

"Not exactly, but a friend of mine had some real trouble with his daughter. After studying the Technique for a few months, Vanessa started mixin' up reality and her actin'. Couldn't tell the difference between pretend and real life after a while." Robb shook his head gravely as he helped Randi out of the harness. "Poor Dave had to have his kid deprogrammed or somethin', just like she was in a weird cult."

"Perhaps her father overreacted."

"Nah, Vanessa needed to have someone tell her how to live her life. The Technique seems to appeal most to immature personalities that can be molded. But you know kids nowadays," he said, his voice rich with the disgust of disappointed parents everywhere. "They never think of turnin' to their own folks for that kind of help."

"I really don't think the Technique is that extreme, at least not for most people," Randi said defensively as they walked to his office. "Both Nora Pratt and Dion Hayden are in T-groups, and *they're* normal."

Or at least Dion is, Randi insisted to herself. There were times when Nora did carry her film role a little too far into her real life, though the actress hadn't done anything really dramatic recently.

"Hey, speakin' of Dion Hayden, how's the ol' boy doin'?"

"He's doing great." Randi hoped the flush brought on by the thought of exactly how great wasn't reflected on her face. "Why do you ask?"

Robb's bushy gray brows furrowed. "Don't you remember I supervised the mechanical gags on *Distant Lightning?* Dion and I got to be pretty chummy, though we weren't as good friends as he and Clarence Daws." Robb referred to the award-winning director of the movie Dion had made the year before.

"So he and Clarence are friends."

"Were. I don't know that they are anymore. I mean not close, anyway." Robb sat behind his desk and propped his feet on its edge. "I saw Clarence a few months ago and asked him how Dion was doin'. Said last time he heard from the golden boy was when he got a birthday card last spring. Well, what do you expect?" he grumbled, furrowing his brow. "This industry is lousy on personal relationships. And both Clarence and Dion have been on location half a world away from each other."

"It's tough all right," Randi said thoughtfully. "Hey listen, Robb. I've got to get going. I've got another appointment."

"It's almost seven o'clock already and you've been here all day!" he chastised her. "Ariadne, you are lookin' after your health, aren't you?"

"Grumble, grumble, grumble. If I didn't know better, Robb Ochs, I'd think my mother had been playing around before I was born." At his horror-stricken look, Randi laughed and added, "I'm only teasing, but it's no less than you deserve for trying to act like my father."

"Ah, get goin'!"

140

Randi blew the older man a kiss as she swept through the door. But once out of the building and heading for her car, her steps slowed and her lighthearted attitude evaporated. Robb's comments had stirred up some old insecurities. *This industry is lousy on personal relationships.* Didn't she know that firsthand from her own childhood?

But her relationship with Dion was different, wasn't it? Dion had insisted that having someone to love was more important than fame and fortune.

With that thought cheering her, Randi climbed into her car and headed for the Hollywood restaurant where she was to meet her lover for dinner in exactly half an hour. Eager to be with him—to see his face light up with a special smile when he saw her—Randi didn't care that she'd be a little early. She'd never mind waiting for Dion.

But when she pulled into the lot of Grayson's and a car jockey opened her door, Randi spotted Dion's car immediately. So he had been as eager to see her as she had been to see him! Grinning broadly, wicked thoughts of the night ahead racing through her mind, Randi entered the restaurant and was greeted by its owner.

"Ah, Ms. St. Martin! I'm sure I can find you an excellent table."

"It's all right, Jack. I'm meeting Dion Hayden. Just point me in the right direction and have the waitress bring me a glass of Perrier with lime."

To Jack's disappointment, Randi insisted on making her way through the dimly lit restaurant to Dion's booth alone. She didn't want a third party intruding on her reunion with her lover. That was why she'd chosen a place with the quiet intimacy of Grayson's.

The place wasn't crowded, and Dion had chosen one of

the booths in back. They'd have enough privacy to satisfy them both, Randi thought happily.

"Shifting Sands sounds exactly right for me. I've always wanted to do a swashbuckling historical."

That was Dion's voice. When she spotted him, Randi could see he wasn't alone, but she couldn't quite make out the identity of his companion. Dion was gazing inward, his expression serious, and Randi heard an unfamiliar male voice speak up.

"When you told me you were interested in this sand epic, I got right on it."

Slowing her steps, Randi was reluctant to interrupt; nor did she want to eavesdrop on what sounded like a business meeting. She checked her watch. Ten minutes early. Maybe she'd better drink her Perrier at the bar, Randi thought, but the man's next words rooted her to the spot.

"This production in North Africa is going to be really big. All the top names in Hollywood and Europe are vying for the lead now that Cami had to pull out because of the car accident. But Rafe Santi wants *you,"* he insisted, referring to Italy's most well-known director.

"I'm flattered, Harold."

Harold. The other man was Dion's agent, Harold Roth, Randi realized.

"When's *Chrysalis* going to be wrapped?"

"The footage should be completed in two weeks, if the weather holds."

"Hm-m. That doesn't give you much leeway if something goes wrong. The cast and crew of *Shifting Sands* has got to be in the desert to shoot by mid-November, but the director wants you in Morocco by the first, if at all possible," Harold told him. "Fittings and rehearsals take time."

Dion was unusually quiet, and Randi held her breath waiting for his answer. Would he take the offer or turn it down? Could he really pack up and leave her after they'd barely admitted their love for each other? Randi stared at Dion's perfect profile and began to miss him already. She knew they'd have to be separated at times because of their careers, but she and Dion hadn't even had a fair chance to work things out between them.

"I'll think about it."

"What's to think? Say yes and I'll have the contracts by the beginning of next week."

"Look, Harold, I'm interested, but there are other considerations. I'll get back to you."

"I know, I know. There's the rest of your contract with the network. Hey, you don't have to worry. I've cleared it already. I played golf with Bob Savage this morning," Harold told him, referring to the network's chairman of the board. "Good thing you guys are buddy-buddy. He'll put the rest of your contract on extension till you get back from North Africa."

"Harold, don't push."

"You're the boss," the agent returned, but he didn't sound pleased. "But Rafe wants a replacement fast."

Trying to decide whether to retreat to the bar or to make herself known, Randi was slightly uneasy when the decision was taken out of her hands. Dion turned his Mediterranean blue gaze in her direction, and she was caught.

"Randi?"

"Hi." She stepped forward into the circle of soft light yet stopped a few feet from the booth. "I—I don't want

143

to interrupt if you're having a meeting. I'm early," she finished lamely.

"Don't be silly," Dion told her, but there was something missing in his welcome—enthusiasm. He patted the seat next to him. "Climb in."

Randi slid next to Dion, though she didn't sit too close. Even so, the sensuality he exuded stirred her. Uneasily she eyed the dark-haired, brown-eyed man on the other side of the table. He'd risen at her approach and now was inspecting her with a disconcerting thoroughness. Did she pass muster? Randi wondered, irritated by his scrutiny. When he held out a hand heavy with gold rings, she shook it, though a bit reluctantly.

"Harold Roth."

He said the name with great assurance, as though she would recognize it in an instant. In fact, until working with Dion, Randi had never heard of him.

"Sorry," Dion said as though waking from a trance. "Randi St. Martin, my agent . . ."

Dressed for success, Harold Roth exuded that sometimes-elusive attribute. From his dark suit complemented by a designer silk tie and diamond stickpin to his hundred-dollar haircut, the agent's demeanor shouted both his affluence and his confidence to the world. For some reason Randi took an instant dislike to the man.

"So you're the famous Randi St. Martin," Harold said, baring his teeth. They were so perfectly straight and white, Randi wondered if they were capped. "The town is agog at your exploits in the wild."

What did *that* mean?

"Ah, we have a business dinner, Harold," Dion cut in smoothly. "Why don't I get back to you?"

The agent still smiled, but his eyes were cold, letting

144

Randi know he didn't like being dismissed on her account.

"Certainly. I'll be waiting for your call," Harold said to Dion as the waitress brought Randi her drink.

Once the man had left, she waited for Dion to explain what his meeting had been about. Disappointed at his introspection—for although he settled an arm around her, Dion seemed disinclined to talk—Randi decided to bring up the subject herself.

"I'm sorry I interrupted your meeting. It sounded like you and Harold had a lot to discuss."

"Don't worry," he answered absently, giving her shoulders a slight squeeze. "It was nothing important."

But Randi knew that it *was* important. He'd told Harold *Shifting Sands* was exactly right for him. He'd said he was interested. He was lying to her. Why?

The doubts raised earlier by Robb Ochs flitted through her mind as they ate dinner, her thoughts only occasionally interrupted by a sliver of conversation. For some reason Dion didn't want her to know about the offer for the lead in *Shifting Sands*. Was he already emotionally withdrawing by excluding her from the important things in his life?

Randi silently scolded herself for being so maudlin. Dion hadn't given Harold the go-ahead, had he? Neither had he turned down the project, her alter ego argued. But if he did decide to take the part, he'd be gone in a flash, immediately after the completion of shooting on *Chrysalis*.

Where did that leave her—them, she corrected—since she'd be left behind during the long editing process.

Randi was determined to find out when Dion came back to her apartment that night. She had to, for the sake

145

of her aching heart. But when they got to the lot and sent the jockey after their cars, Dion revealed other plans.

"Listen, Foxy, I'm bushed. You wouldn't mind too much if I didn't come home with you tonight?"

Not ready to hear the real reason, Randi fibbed, "Of course not." Then, "Surely you're not thinking of driving all the way home if you're that tired?"

"No. I thought I'd stay at my parents' place."

"Oh."

"Hey," he said softly, lifting her chin for a quick kiss. "You know if I go home with you neither of us will get much sleep."

"That's true."

"Then kiss me good night as if you mean it."

Randi kissed him with a mixture of tenderness and passion, trying to make him understand how much he meant to her. Dion returned the embrace, and she heard him moan as he clasped her body to his own. Was he about to change his mind?

"Hey folks, your cars?" Randi and Dion pulled apart quickly at the young man's words, but still each stared into the other's face. Was Dion's expression a little sad? The car jockey continued. "There are other people waiting for their vehicles."

"Sorry," Randi apologized as she and Dion parted.

He waved to her at the exit, where they turned in opposite directions. Randi threw Dion a kiss and whispered a good-bye that she hoped wasn't a prophecy for their future.

It was *hot*. Death Valley, the lowest point in the Mojave Desert, surrounded by salt-encrusted playas, drifting dunes, multicolored canyons and austere mountains, was a potential death trap for the unwary. Randi had chosen to save the desert sequences until last, because October in Death Valley was supposed to be comfortably warm. Unfortunately, the intense summer heat had lingered long after temperatures should have dropped to the eighties or lower.

It *had* been 80 when they'd risen at four-thirty, Randi assured herself—she'd checked upon leaving her motel room—but now, approaching ten A.M., it was 98 degrees. Of course, it could have been worse. Knowing they were lucky not to experience July temperatures, which could reach 120 and higher, was not much of a consolation, however.

The unexpected heat wave adversely affected the small cast and crew of *Chrysalis*. The off-worlders Lara, Reed and Mallory were being led by Shann to a sacred place that held the key to the planet's civilization. But each morning, within hours of the first setup, thirst became a continual problem and tempers flared with little provocation.

"Damnit, Nora, what's wrong with you, anyway?"

"Paul, please! Give me a break! Stop being so pushy."

"I thought you said you loved me?" Silence. Then his voice rose even higher. "So what's the problem all of a sudden?"

As Randi sat atop a sand dune under the dubious shade of a scrawny mesquite while checking her shooting script, she tried to block out their squabbling.

"I'm just not sure we're right for each other."

"It's that damn T-group!"

"Leave my acting method out of this!"

"Why should I? Are you leaving it out of our lives? Or have you brought your role into our relationship? You

147

don't really care about me, but Reed and Mallory love each other. Are you living your part? Have you been acting all this time?"

Paul's words chilled Randi, because they forced her to face something she'd been avoiding for the past week: what if Dion had brought *his* role as a lover into their relationship?

Nora burst into tears. "I don't know anything anymore. To tell you the truth, Paul, right now I don't see there's much about you to love!"

Sobbing, she ran to the makeup trailer, with Paul following right behind her. "Nora, listen, please." The blonde slammed the door in his face.

Randi couldn't say she hadn't been warned about the effects of the Technique. Robb's words haunted her. Dion had had a close relationship with his director Clarence Daws, and now he had one, albeit of a different sort, with her. Hadn't she heard Sally gossiping about it? Did Dion make it a point to get close to all his directors—until the shoot ended? Once he left for his next location, would *she* receive only a birthday card from him before he forgot her altogether?

Since the dinner at Grayson's, they'd spent only one night together, and it had been a bittersweet experience, different from their previous lovemaking, in which passion had been mixed with laughter. Randi decided part of the problem was hers. In getting ready for the final shoot, she hadn't had much time for Dion. Now she wondered if it mattered to him.

"Hey, Randi, Chuck's set up."

"Good, Jake." Randi forced a smile for her assistant. "Why don't you see if Nora will be able to do her scene?"

"Check."

Thank goodness Jake had turned out to be an all right person once he loosened up and accepted her—a woman —as his director. She'd relied on him heavily during the last few tense days.

Hearing a rustling behind her, Randi jumped. A sidewinder? she wondered, heart pounding. Checking carefully, she found nothing. Of course not! she scolded herself. The desert creatures were nocturnal. Unlike crazy humans, they knew better than to come out to bake their brains in the sun.

That was her problem, Randi decided. She was letting the heat get to her. Dion loved her as much as she did him, but they were both tired and had other things on their minds. Everything would straighten out once they moved on to the cooler high Mojave.

Somehow everyone got through several more days of shooting in various parts of Death Valley without a major confrontation, but while temperatures at their next destination were at least ten degrees cooler, the heat wave continued. No one was in a particularly good mood, especially after the generator that ran the air-conditioning for their trailers broke down in the middle of the night.

Just before sunrise the first morning after their move to the new location, Randi looked out at one of the most incredible landscapes in the California desert: the Devil's Playground, its desolate, windswept plain giving way to the Kelso Sand Dunes. Sand flats scattered with creosote bushes and galleta grass rose to mountains of tawny white granite particles, their beauty accented by the streaked early morning sky.

"Fabulous," she whispered, sure this was the perfect setting for the important love scene between Shann and Lara. There in the dunes, after finding the remains of the

149

spaceship *Chrysalis,* they would realize they were of the same origin: Earth. With that fact Lara would finally be able to accept her love for Shann as well as the psychic powers that drew them together.

"Johnson said the wreck is set," Jake said from behind.

Randi turned to her assistant. "Good. Are the jeeps ready to take the equipment across?"

"All set."

"Then start loading. Chuck," she called to her cameraman. He ambled over to her, his almost perpetual insolent expression in place. "Set up just this side of the wreck," Randi told him, referring to the initial camera placement.

"Are you sure, boss lady? Is that *exactly* how your godmother Olga would prefer the scene shot?"

"Just do it!" Randi ordered.

Spinning on her heel, she headed for the trailers. Dion was the only one who could have told Chuck that Olga was her godmother. And she had trusted him to keep her confidence!

Another suspicion quickly formed. How could Randi have forgotten his agent's claim that Dion was buddy-buddy with network chief Bob Savage? Early in the shoot she'd thought Jake had the ear of the network execs. Had it been Dion who passed on every piece of gossip? The warnings issued from Benny had stopped once she and Dion had gotten personally involved. That realization seemed to clinch Dion's guilt.

With the clang of metal in the background—the air-conditioning was not yet restored—Dion's and Jocelyn's voices drifted from the makeup trailer, where he seemed to be coaching the actress.

"You've got to sink into your feelings, Jocelyn. Adapt yourself within the confines of your character."

Randi stopped short, wanting to hear Dion coach Jocelyn.

"What do you mean?" Jocelyn asked.

"Lara is from an emotionally isolated background and she allows Shann to discover both her warmth and something deeper: a psychic bond. At first Lara is distrustful of this younger man who depends on his own feelings rather than technical knowledge. Shann is attracted to Lara because he respects her integrity and courage."

Stunned, Randi realized Dion could easily be talking about their own personal relationship.

"I've gone over all this in my mind, Dion, but I'm still not comfortable with it. I've gotten into the straighter, more rigid side of Lara, but I'm not sure I can switch over so easily into the part of her personality that allows her to change."

"Have fun with it. Let go. Think of the times Shann has played with Lara, whether or not she played back. He's teased her, nurtured her, challenged her. In this last scene let Lara remember, and she'll naturally respond."

Randi didn't want to hear any more. Unknowingly Dion had hit her where she was most vulnerable, and she hated the feeling. Especially now, when she was beginning to understand the illusion. Dion might remain the golden god of Hollywood, but in her heart the idol was crumbling!

"Are you two ready for your scene?" she called from where she stood.

"Randi."

His voice was soft, and as Dion stuck his head outside the trailer, his eyes caressed her as intimately as they'd ever done. Was he gearing up for the big love scene by practicing on her? Randi wondered bitterly.

"I'll be waiting for you at the jeep."

The morning did not go well. Randi tried to remain cool and professional, but it was only with great restraint that she didn't lose her temper. No matter how many takes they shot, Jocelyn couldn't make the personality change believable.

"Randi, I'm sorry, but it's impossible the way you've blocked it," Jocelyn complained, referring to the physical movement of the actors in the scene. "I can't concentrate on keeping my footing in the shifting sand and on changing my personality gradually too."

"You can do it," Randi encouraged the actress for at least the tenth time. "Think about it before you begin. You move around this wreck, making one discovery after another. The name on the hull hits you first: *Chrysalis,* an English word. An important bond is forged between you and Shann when you realize you're both descendants of Earth explorers."

The light would change soon, Randi realized. In half an hour, as the sun rose high in the late morning sky, it would cast deep shadows and ruin the soft effect she wanted. The morning would be wasted.

Tapping the reserves of her patience, Randi continued. "Now you know Shann's culture is not as strange and forbidding as you've convinced yourself. So with each step you take, each new discovery you make, the veil drops and your heightened perception shows you your relationship as it really is. Finally you allow your psychic bond free reign so you can hear his thoughts: he loves you."

"But why do I have to keep moving?"

"Because the restless energy is natural to you. Shann is emotionally centered. When something bothers you, emotions emerge and you react physically."

"I'll try."

But she didn't succeed, not after three more takes.

"Again," Randi said relentlessly, sure Jocelyn could do it.

"I can't!"

"You can!"

"Randi," Dion interrupted. "Maybe if we changed the blocking . . ."

"The blocking stays!"

"You're being inflexible," Dion softly insisted.

Randi couldn't believe it. Dion was backing Jocelyn *again!* It was as if, once immersed in his role, Dion switched his affections from his real life to his screen lover! From the corner of her eye she spied Jake, waiting for her instructions.

"Jake, what do you think?" Randi asked, sure he was her ally.

Hesitating for a moment, Jake reluctantly agreed. "Maybe they're right. Jocelyn may do better with simple blocking."

"What is this? A conspiracy?"

"Randi!" Dion's tone made her uncomfortable. "We're trying to solve the problem!"

"The problem is my concern. I'm the director," Randi snapped, finally losing all patience. "The scene stays. Since the sun's too high to shoot it now, you might as well practice. Maybe she'll come around with your special coaching *technique.* We'll try to shoot it in the morning!"

With that she walked off, jumped into one of the jeeps

and ignored Dion's final "Randi!" as she ordered the driver, Eddie, to take her back to her trailer. Glancing back, she saw Dion commandeer the other jeep to follow.

As the wheels of the jeep spun, then gripped the loose terrain, a cloud of dust surrounded Randi and her driver. Sand blew in their faces until they were both coughing. Randi held on, giving the driver his due: he would have made a New York cabbie green with envy.

Checking on Dion, she realized his jeep was gaining on theirs. She turned forward to peer out the dust-laden windshield.

A miniforest of creosote bushes was no obstacle to Eddie's talented curves and swerves. Randi hung on for dear life. A scarred snout weevil interrupted its mid-morning snack to dart for cover, and a half-grown rabbit, its nap disturbed, jumped from its green-leaved shelter in panic, nearly hopping under the jeep's wheels.

When she spied the trailers, hitched in a circle as if to fight off the marauding Indians in a low-budget western, Randi glanced back at Dion once more. He was still following, but at a more reasonable pace. For some reason he'd lost the urge to keep up with her.

"Here you go, Ms. St. Martin," Eddie said, bringing the jeep to a halt. "Boy, that was fun! I don't often get the chance to drive like that."

Randi strode to her trailer, hesitating when she saw an anxious uniformed messenger with a large manila envelope in hand.

"I'm Randi St. Martin. Is that for me?"

"No. Dion Hayden. I've got some important contracts his agent wants signed, and I've been waiting for half an hour already."

154

"All right, Randi . . ." she heard a masculine voice say from several yards away.

"Here's Mr. Hayden now."

Randi stalked off in anger, sure she knew exactly what contracts the messenger was carrying.

"Mr. Hayden, Harold Roth sent me with these papers."

"Come into my trailer," Dion said curtly. "I need a chance to cool off!"

Once in her own trailer, now suitably cool since the generator had been repaired, Randi paced the half-dozen steps the limited space would allow. Glancing at her reflection in a small mirror hung on the back of the door, she stopped and stared in amazement at the sand-encrusted woman glaring back at her.

Wiping her face with both hands, Randi forced them to her sides. Who cared?

Sure that Dion would follow as soon as he signed the contracts that would take him to North Africa, Randi wondered if she should answer when he banged on her door. She vacillated between opening it, telling him exactly what she thought of his interference, and then slamming the door in his face and allowing him to stand out in the sun to broil to death!

It was a long time before Randi realized Dion wasn't about to come knocking.

CHAPTER TEN

In the golden light of late afternoon, the southern California landscape looked as surrealistic as a hand-painted photograph. Driving toward Pasadena, Randi thought she'd never seen so many strange pink Spanish-style motels.

Dion stared out the window, maintaining a stern and distant profile, surveying the passing scenery while ignoring her. Randi wasn't surprised. Dion probably was contemplating the film to be shot in North Africa. He wouldn't need her now that *Chrysalis* and the bond between Shann and Lara had both evolved and ended.

Uncomfortable with the continuing silence but unwilling to talk, Randi switched on the car radio to a soft rock station.

"Could you turn that down, please?"

Angry at Dion's neutral tone, Randi did as he asked. They'd rarely spoken since their wild chase across the desert floor, and she was gearing herself up to tell him what she thought of his interference.

Determinedly, Randi had refused to give up her principles, so she'd kept the crew a few days later than planned, going over budget to get the performance she wanted from Jocelyn. Her single-mindedness had paid off. The lead actress had come through, just as Randi had known was possible.

Dion hadn't seemed appreciative, but at least he'd done his job without complaint, repeating Shann's lines over and over in the desert's blinding light. Relieved, Randi had carefully kept her distance from him, busying herself each time she'd caught him staring at her.

On the bus trip back to Los Angeles, she'd maneuvered herself into a seat next to Nora. The supporting actress's subdued demeanor—she'd broken up with Paul, it seemed—suitably matched Randi's mood.

Then, once they were back in L.A., she'd found Dion waiting against her car in the production company's parking lot. Since his car was parked in a garage near her condo, he'd assumed she'd give him a ride. Randi had been tempted to tell him to take a cab.

"We'll be at my place in a couple of minutes," she said with a disinterest she was far from feeling.

"Uh-huh."

Bitterness welling in her, Randi blinked away the tears pricking her eyes. When Dion left her this time, she might never see him again. If only she could dismiss him as easily as he would her. But *she* wasn't shallow and immature!

"I thought you'd have worked out your anger by now," Dion said with a sigh, turning toward her and placing an arm on the back of the seat. "I've waited and given you plenty of space. I shouldn't have interfered with your directions about that scene no matter what I thought, but I figured we could talk about it."

He caressed her shoulder lightly, and Randi's anger flared at his touch. Why couldn't he just say good-bye?

Anything else would prolong her agony. Wanting to lash out at him, she kept her voice even and controlled.

"Here we are," she said, pulling up to his car. "You can get out now. Our little affair is over." He seemed surprised, she thought with satisfaction. "I have my own directorial *technique,* Dion. To get the best out of my lead actors, I make love to them. Since the miniseries is over, you can take your pretty face elsewhere."

Dion's jaw dropped, but she had to admit he pulled himself together admirably.

"Do you expect me to believe that?"

"I expect you to get out of this car!"

"And I'm not going anywhere until you stop this! I don't know why you're acting crazy, but it doesn't become you."

Frustrated because she'd failed, Randi blurted, "I guess I should have gotten into one of your T-groups so I could deliver lines as smoothly as you do."

Dion frowned in confusion. "What's all *this* about?"

"Don't ask me. *You're* the one who's involved with an acting method that encourages people to mix fantasy with real life!"

"I think you'd better explain that remark."

"Was it a coincidence you pursued me? Or did you plan it after reading the script so you could prepare for your role? The similarity of the real and filmed situations is amazing! Think of how well Lara's and my views of life coincide: immersed in technical detail, strangers to our own emotions." Silently she added how they'd both fallen in love with the same man, Dion and his alter ego Shann. "They say that art mirrors life, but when it's the other way around, there's something wrong."

She remembered other "mirroring" that, at the time,

had seemed like coincidence. Dion had made a grand entrance at Olga's similar to the gate scene in *Chrysalis*. Then there had been the pool scenes in the wild and at his ranch, both of which had led to a more intimate relationship between Dion and his filmed and real-life women.

Randi went on. "I think you've immersed yourself in a character and carried him into your life—my life too. I suppose your method has succeeded for you. You've put in a great performance, Dion. However, as far as I'm concerned, you've been emotionally irresponsible!"

"I'm sorry you feel that way."

His calmness made Randi defend herself further. "You can't deny you've repeated lines to me that you've spoken in movies: *'Live for the moment.' 'The most important thing in life is having someone to love.' 'We're poetry together.'* You said that to me after the initial production meeting at Olga's house. Did you think I wouldn't recognize them?" When he didn't answer, Randi queried, "Do you remember saying the words?"

"I remember."

"Well, good! Maybe you'll also remember telling Chuck Brockman that Olga is my godmother. How else did he find out? Only you knew that. And you promised not to tell!"

"I didn't say anything to him."

Why didn't he jump to defend himself? Randi wondered. Was he telling the literal truth while lying by omission? Had he spoken to certain network people who, in turn, had informed Chuck?

"How do I know who you really are? Or who you're playing?" she asked him. "Did you adopt your charming facade from your Technique classes? Underneath, are you

159

the same insecure, vain actor you were three years ago? Your behavior on and off the set doesn't exactly typify an integrated personality."

Dion's face reddened. Now she'd made him angry!

"I hope you're having a good time dissecting me, Randi. What horrible things have I done to warrant all this hostility?"

"Maybe you don't know the meaning of reality, Dion, but you'd better realize you can hurt people!" Feeling her throat constrict, Randi struggled to keep herself from crying, especially when she saw the hurt reflected on his face. Another act? She slapped the steering wheel sharply with one hand in order to release her building tension. "Go on to your next project and to your next director and get chummy with him. But do me a favor and don't bother sending me a birthday card!"

When Dion didn't get out of the car, she glared at him.

"Where the hell has all this come from?" he asked finally.

"It's been building up in me for a long time. I ignored my suspicions—closed my ears to what people said about you—made excuses for you. But finally I had to face the facts."

"And you couldn't face *me* with such grave doubts? You thought I was a royal jerk but you pretended we had a good relationship anyway? You're supposed to be a forthright person. To think I respected your honesty and integrity! Talk about being real!"

"Is that your best defense?" Randi asked sadly. "An offense against me?"

Gathering his duffel bag from the rear seat, Dion faced her angrily, his blue eyes blazing. "I wouldn't think of defending myself against such childish accusations!" Be-

160

fore she could object—it wasn't she who was childish—he said, "I'll get out of your life if you want, Randi. You're not the only one who feels betrayed. You said you loved me. I thought you trusted me. And now this! I don't know who *you* are!" Slamming the door as he exited, Dion turned back to shout through the open window. "If you get over your insanity or heat stroke or whatever abnormality it is that's ailing you—and if you can think of a *really* good explanation—give me a call!"

"Do they have phones in the wilds of North Africa?" Randi yelled in return.

Not waiting for an answer, she floored the accelerator and the car leaped away, her stomach lurching with it.

"Olga's upstairs working," Raoul told Randi. "Go on up. She's eager to hear how everything went."

Randi smiled at him as she headed up the marble staircase. "Thanks."

Pausing when she reached the landing, Randi pulled a chocolate cookie from the half-empty package in her purse and stuffed it into her mouth. Suddenly ashamed at her furtive attempt at oral gratification, she fastened the purse securely and promised herself to throw away the rest when she got home.

Moping around her condo after her confrontation with Dion, she'd had trouble finding the energy to do anything. When Olga phoned, Randi had looked forward to a change of scenery.

It was time she quit rehashing the sordid details of her broken love affair. Placing the facts in various configurations hadn't made her thoughts any more clear. She still didn't know whether Dion was for real or not.

The main thing that haunted her was his reaction to

her accusations. He'd have had no precedent with which to identify, no time to rehearse. Yet although he'd been angry with her, he'd remained nondefensive. He'd said that she'd betrayed him, and there'd been an expression of pain on his face. That had been real.

Could the fact that he'd quoted lines from movies have been a coincidence, something any actor might do and still mean what he said?

"Olga?" she called into her godmother's elaborate bedroom.

The only living creature present was one of Olga's seven cats, lying like a king in the center of the huge canopied bed. Randi crossed the oriental carpet to scratch the striped cat under his chin.

"Hello, Kahn, you little devil."

The room was truly a place fit for royalty. In her usual exotic style, Olga had fitted her bed with a Chinese palace tent of embroidered tasseled panels. Above the headboard—padded with tiger-striped velvet—Arabic grillwork was backed by a mirror.

Randi started when she saw herself.

As bad as she looked, she hoped she could fool her eagle-eyed godmother by saying she was tired. Not wanting to discuss Dion, Randi took a calming breath before passing the gold-hinged treasure chest, its top displaying a stained glass lamp, the design depicting a phoenix rising from the flames, surrounded by part of Olga's miniature winged horse collection.

Finding the narrow door in the corner of the room, she ascended the winding steps that led up to Olga's writing tower. She was certain to find the older woman at work on her word processer. Olga didn't look up as Randi entered the small circular room. Her back to the entry-way, she was busy switching off the disk drives.

"Hello, darling! I felt your presence."

"Or heard me coming," Randi said with amusement.

Swinging around in her steno chair, Olga rose to give Randi a hug. "What's the matter? You look terrible!"

"I'm a little tired."

"Did something go wrong on location? I told those idiots not to mess with your direction when they approached me about the name change."

"There were some problems, but I fixed them," Randi fibbed, confining her remarks to her professional difficulties. "I'll be fine once I get a few days' rest."

Olga's narrowed dark eyes told Randi the woman didn't believe her. Fancying herself psychic, Olga could be unnervingly intuitive.

"You'll like the desert scenes," Randi went on quickly, before her godmother could begin an inquisition. "The light was perfect, and I got a splendid performance from Jocelyn."

After hesitating a second, Olga asked, "How about Dion Hayden?"

"He was fine."

"He wasn't troublesome?"

Randi took a deep breath and said, perhaps a little too quickly, "He's picked up a lot of acting skills in three years. It was easy to get what I wanted from him."

Professionally, that is, Randi silently amended.

Olga drew out a chair from the single curving wall. "Off, Hades!" At her imperious command, a black cat scurried from his resting place. "Sit and I'll make you some tea, Randi."

Olga reached for a china pot sitting on its matching

163

hot-plate holder. Watching her godmother mix and measure the tea with sugar into tiny cups, Randi was reminded of an alchemist at work. The setting was right: a tower room, leering gargoyles serving as bookends for aged volumes, a collection of antique blown glass, rich colors vibrating against the flesh-colored walls. And, dressed in a hooded dark brown caftan with bell sleeves, her silver hair plaited and looped around her ears, was Olga herself.

It did seem as if she might be concocting potions in her magical tower, Randi fancied. Although she knew Olga would like the analogy, she had no intention of voicing the thought.

"Thanks," Randi said as she accepted a cup of tea.

Sitting at her writing desk, Olga said, "Now, tell me what is wrong."

"Nothing."

"Nonsense. I've known all your moods since the day you were born—no, before."

Having been her mother's best friend and writing partner—they'd co-authored a fantasy novel before Emily went into scriptwriting—Olga claimed she'd known Randi's sex and personality before she was born.

"You're imagining things," Randi bluffed.

"Does your lack of sleep have something to do with Dion Hayden? Have you gotten involved with him again?"

Randi sighed. What had she expected? Her godmother was relentless. "For a short time. But now I'm uninvolved. I came here to talk about the miniseries, not Dion."

"What happened?"

164

"I got all the footage I wanted, though the production ran a few days over budget. But that's a minor—"

"With you and Dion, darling."

Randi capitulated. "We aren't right for each other. He's an actor. *Always!*"

" 'All the world's a stage!' " Olga quoted.

"I don't like his characters. They're too shallow."

"Really? Are you sure you're not upholding your parents' prejudice?" Olga put aside her teacup. "They're so conservative now. Except for their movie scripts, of course."

"I'm not conservative!"

"M-m-m. Yes, well, I like Dion." Olga went on. "I was impressed when he came to speak to me about being cast as Shann. From what you'd told me, I expected an offensive egotist. Instead I met an intelligent, sincere young man who'd read my book and asked creative questions. He was not shallow, Ariadne."

Randi took notice of the proper name Olga used only when she was upset with her goddaughter. Becoming miffed herself, Randi asked, "Are you sure you didn't form your opinion of Dion because he admired your book so much?"

"Of course not. I'm not blinded by flattery. I don't know what happened between the two of you this time, but I think you should reconsider. You sound very judgmental to me."

"Olga?" Raoul's voice and the sound of his steps echoed up the stairwell, interrupting Randi's reply. Olga's remarks hadn't helped her self-doubts. The fact that her godmother had a talent for understanding people made Randi doubly uncomfortable.

Could she have been so totally mistaken? She should

have questioned Dion about her suspicions long ago, but Randi had been distrustful of her own instincts. Honesty in her work was simple, but in complex romantic relationships it wasn't so easy.

"I'm going to retire now." Raoul kissed his slightly taller wife affectionately. Awakening in the afternoon and working at night, Olga kept a schedule opposite that of her early-rising husband. "We can discuss the Halloween party tomorrow at dinner."

"I'll be looking forward to it, my love. Sweet dreams!" Olga called after him as Raoul left for his own quarters in the lower half of the mansion. Looking back at Randi, Olga stated, "Unusual women need unusual men."

"If they can find them," Randi agreed, impressed as always by Olga and Raoul's idealized romantic love for each other after twenty years of marriage. "I've always thought you and Raoul were lucky."

"I am blessed, but I also have good judgment," Olga said, irritating Randi as she prepared herself for a lecture. "And so do you, if you'd listen to your intuitive side. You're willing to take risks in your work but not with your personal life. I've noticed you've always chosen men who were so safe, they weren't even interesting."

Randi opened her mouth to protest, but Olga went on without giving her the opportunity.

"Now Dion Hayden, on the other hand, is extremely interesting. I thought he was perfect for the role of Shann. He's so warm, capable of being able to nurture and yet challenge the woman he loves. I also thought Dion Hayden was right for you."

"So you thought you'd play matchmaker by recommending him?"

"I would have agreed to his playing the role anyway,"

166

Olga said. "But since you still cared, I was sure the elemental forces would take their natural course."

"Storms and volcanic eruptions?" Leave it to her godmother to know all her secrets! Randi fumed.

"I mean personality traits that complement each other. You're intense, while Dion is easygoing. You lean toward your intellect, and he leans toward his emotions. You're individualistic and he's cooperative. A very fine combination."

"I'm glad you thought it all out."

"Don't be sarcastic. I'm interested in your happiness. You need a man like Dion if you're to marry and still become a top director."

"You thought we'd get married?"

"I had certain feelings."

Here was the psychic stuff again! Randi dearly loved Olga, but the older woman annoyed her when she tried to play the part of a seer. "Your intuition is often right, but in this case I want to work out the details myself."

"Of course," Olga immediately agreed as though knowing when to back off.

Peering at her godmother with suspicion—had Olga's retreat been too hasty?—Randi said, "I sincerely appreciate your advice and I'll let you know how things go." Then she firmly steered the discussion to the miniseries.

She wasn't ready to share her deepest hurt and doubt yet, or her hopes for the future. With surprise, Randi recognized that she *did* have hope. Now that she'd thought things over—with a little help from her fairy godmother—Randi realized that only a calm discussion with Dion would clear the air. And he had told her to call him if she wanted to talk, Randi remembered.

Olga was staring at her, a knowing smile on her lips.

Randi realized she'd stopped her business discussion in the middle of a sentence. Quickly she tried to cover by asking, "Are you coming down to the studio to view some of the scenes before they're edited?"

"I plan to," Olga told her. "After I recover from our annual Halloween fete, that is. The theme this year is mystical creatures and beings. Have you decided on a costume?"

"I've been so busy, I forgot," Randi said with genuine disappointment. "I don't have a suitable costume." Olga's Halloween parties were fabulous festivals not to be missed.

"You're welcome to borrow something from me."

"Olga, I greatly doubt any of your treasures would fit me," Randi protested, looking up at the woman who was almost four inches taller and two sizes smaller than she.

"We'll see. Come downstairs. I may have a dress that will be perfect."

Randi followed her godmother down the steps and into a closet almost as big as her own bedroom. In rows on narrow rods, Olga's collection of exotic clothes hung in colorful display.

"Here it is."

Without having to search for it, Olga found and held out a beautifully simple dress. Cream-colored and vertically pleated with tiny folds, it reminded Randi of the work of the designer Fortuny. The garment was sleeveless and had a low, draped neckline. The sides fastened with small hooks and eyes from underarm to knee.

"It's beautiful!"

"It's in the tradition of a Greek chiton, only more clinging and flattering. You can leave the hooks unfastened as far up as you dare. With your figure, you'll look like a goddess. H-m-m." Olga paused. "You'll have to go to the party as your namesake, Ariadne."

It was too perfect, Randi suspected as she gratefully accepted the dress, sure Olga had purchased it specially for her. Randi was equally sure Olga knew that Dion's name was a shortened version of *Dionysus.* Wouldn't her godmother love to set them up as the mythological couple? That must mean Olga was sure Dion would come to her party, Randi thought excitedly.

Thanking Olga after accepting some jewelry from the older woman's collection, Randi hugged her and left. If nothing else, Olga was always concerned about her godchild, she thought, almost skipping down the marble stairs.

Being truthful with herself, Randi admitted why she'd come to the mansion so eagerly: she'd wanted to hear what Olga had to say about Dion Hayden. And her godmother had forced Randi to reevaluate her doubts about the man she loved. Guilt had germinated the moment Dion walked away from the car, but it had taken Randi a few days to come to terms with her mistake and the reason for it: She'd always balked at recognizing the strength and wisdom of her inner self.

Randi had tried to push Dion away because he stirred her strongest feelings and she didn't know how to cope with an intangible. She'd exaggerated their problems and had allowed outsiders to influence the way she saw him. She'd been wrong about his character. But what about the future of their relationship?

If Dion truly cared, as Randi now believed, even a separation of several months, like for the movie in Africa, couldn't destroy what they felt for each other.

But would their love last for an eternity?

Randi had to laugh at her own ridiculousness. How could a mere mortal answer that? In any relationship there were risks. Randi was now willing to take them.

And this visit had made Randi realize she *had* had experience with a deep emotional attachment that had lasted for thirty-four years—with Olga. Romance added a heightened dimension to commitment, but suddenly it didn't seem beyond her capacities.

Going out through the central hallway, Randi stopped at a small cupboard door. Behind it, a telephone was set in an alcove. Quickly dialing Dion's number, she counted the rings, then was startled when a strange female voice answered.

"Mr. Hayden's residence. Can I take a message?"

"Is Dion there?"

"I can't give you that information. This is his answering service."

"Is he gone? When is he coming back?"

"I can only take a message."

"Never mind."

She hung up. Had Dion already left for North Africa? Randi wondered sadly, holding the precious costume to her chest. If so, it was her fault that they hadn't worked things out in time. Perhaps he had truly loved her, but she'd driven him away with her hurtful accusations.

Filled with regret that she'd come to her senses too late, Randi opened the heavy front door and walked out into the lonely night.

CHAPTER ELEVEN

Randi wound her way through the throng of lushly costumed people. A bird-man's feathers tickled her nose, distracting her so she bumped into a golden sphinx.

"Sorry," Randi apologized, but the beautiful black woman stared at her haughtily before turning back to her companion.

Creatures and strange beings from myth, legend and outer space milled around the balcony and scattered throughout the garden below. The Halloween celebration was doubling as a cast party for *Chrysalis,* so the miniseries cast and crew were sure to be here.

Except Dion, Randi thought sadly. Although she'd tried, she'd never reached her lover. She'd miss him tonight, but Randi wouldn't renounce their love—not even if she had to fly to North Africa to recapture the magic! In the meantime she intended to celebrate the lively holiday with friends.

Peering around hopefully, Randi stopped in the center of Olga's two-story drawing room, disappointed when she saw no one she knew. The closely packed crowd made finding friends and acquaintances difficult. Masks and paint hid any familiar faces. Her search was futile.

A man dressed as Captain Hook returned her glance

171

with an admiring leer. Conscious of her low neckline and her leg bared to the thigh, she moved away. *Really!* Randi thought as she escaped, this wasn't supposed to be a *Star Wars* pickup bar!

"Ouch! Watch your big feet!"

In her bemusement Randi had tripped over a midget. "Did I hurt you?" She reached down to help him, but the little man scurried away to join the other six miniacrobats who'd come to the gathering with a woman dressed as Snow White.

"Randi!" a familiar voice called, and she turned toward Flash Gordon and Dale Arden as they came down the stairs. "No! Over here!"

A long, slim arm beckoned to her over several heads. Randi pushed her way to a woman dressed in a leopardskin with armbands and ankle bracelets of animal teeth. It took her a moment to recognize the face beneath the flowing blond wig. "Jocelyn?"

"Call me Sheena, Queen of the Jungle, tonight," Jocelyn said with a laugh. "And this gorgeous lion is Matt."

Randi shook the large paw presented to her and noted the friendly brown eyes behind the mask. "Hi, Matt."

"I was hoping to see you so I could thank you for the extra coaching you gave me," Jocelyn told Randi. "I was so tired after the desert scenes, I didn't get a chance. You've got tremendous patience. Because of it, I feel like a professional actress rather than a model mouthing lines. I'm truly grateful."

Touched by the tribute, which made the extra work worthwhile, Randi smiled warmly. "I couldn't have done it if you hadn't had the ability in you."

The lion was tugging on Sheena's arm and gesturing

172

wildly. "What? Food? You quarterbacks are always hungry!" Jocelyn turned to Randi. "I hope he can get this mask off to eat or he's going to be in a terrible mood!"

Following in the couple's wake, Randi headed toward the long buffet table bordering one end of the room. Decorated with sheaves of wheat and orange candles, it was heaped with food. When Randi looked at the appealing spread—sweetbreads, vegetables with dip, meats and cheeses along with apples and pomegranates—she was surprised that she wasn't hungry. Was it because she was finally satisfied with herself and felt outwardly beautiful?

Wanting only a cool drink, Randi's eyes gravitated to the punch bowl, then widened.

"Chaos!" Randi hissed. Olga's calico cat was calmly lapping at the orange liquid. Hoping no one else had noticed, Randi jostled her way to the bowl, grabbed the cat and put her on the floor. "Chaos, be a good girl! Go play!"

When Randi rose, she saw Chuck Brockman across the tabletop, a set of curving silver horns adorning his head. What was he dressed as, Randi wondered? A minotaur? The bull-type image fit his surly disposition.

Helping herself to some punch, Randi stepped back from the table and bumped into a bearded magician.

"Ah, Ariadne. You must see my new trick—uh, feat of magic." Robb Ochs moved a blue bespangled arm in a sweeping gesture, and several small white furry objects fell to the floor.

A young woman dressed as a unicorn retrieved them. "Here's your rabbits, mister."

"They aren't rabbits. They're creatures. I'm a magician from another world." Robb showed the stuffed toys to Randi. "To tell you the truth, I don't know what these are. Grover made them for me," he said, referring to another of the special effects staff. "Said they'd be more interestin' when I did the sleeve trick."

Randi examined the creatures. "Purple eyes and long toes. They're cute."

"Are your parents here tonight?"

"They don't like this kind of party. . . ." Glancing up, Randi realized Robb was regarding her revealing dress with blatant disapproval. Had she been too daring, wearing nothing beneath it but flesh-colored bikinis? "I'm old enough to be out by myself, Robb."

Reluctantly he smiled, lifting his gaze to her upswept curls caught in a thin gold diadem. "You look beautiful, Ariadne. I forget you're a full-grown woman sometimes. That's some dress!"

"Hey, Randi!" Chuck Brockman ambled past them, his plate loaded with food. "Does your godmother always give such great cast parties?"

Randi was silent as he kept walking.

Robb looked decidedly uncomfortable. "I hope he hasn't been a problem," Robb said. "I sort of told Chuck about Olga and you without thinkin' about it. I guess I should have kept my mouth shut."

So that was how Chuck had obtained his information! Randi thought. "It could have gotten around anyway. You know this business."

"I guess I have a big mouth."

"And a sleeve full of strange creatures!" Randi said, lighthearted, as Robb left to show his trick to another friend.

When Randi put down her glass, Sally Brown was helping herself to the punch. The woman was dressed as Cinderella, wearing an exact replica of the full-skirted

174

blue dress from the Disney movie. Was she looking for Prince Charming? Randi wondered as Sally gave her a syrupy smile.

"Randi!" The high-pitched squeal came from Nora, who pounced on Randi with an enthusiastic hug, almost knocking her into a wall. Nora's pink tulle ballerina skirt and matching wings pricked Randi's skin. "I'm sorry I was so grouchy on the way back to the studio. Paul and I had had a fight. Sometimes I get *so* intense!"

"Yeah." Placing his arm around Nora, Paul said, "Me and the sugar plum fairy here made up, though. Hope we didn't cause you too many problems on the set."

"You both put in outstanding performances."

"Thanks. Now I'm helping Nora get more down to earth."

"And I'm helping Paul be more positive!" Nora chimed in. "I made him dress as an elf for this party."

"I'm an Italian leprechaun," Paul objected, indicating his green tunic and tights. Then he gave a low whistle as he spied the thigh-high cut of Randi's dress. "Boy, do you look gorgeous! A Greek goddess, huh?"

"That costume is perfect on you," Nora agreed. Then she handed her empty plate to Paul. "Will you get me some more fruit?" When he walked away, she drew close to Randi. "Is everything okay with you? On the bus I noticed you were quiet. Was my bad mood catching or did it have something to do with Dion? I know how men *always* cause problems. If you need someone to talk to, I volunteer. I'd like to be your friend."

"I appreciate that." Randi hugged Nora this time. "Consider us friends. But I'm definitely okay, so don't worry. Why don't you help Paul handle all that food. I want to see if I can find Jake," Randi told her.

"Bye!" Nora replied.

Randi moved through the crowd fairly quickly, considering that her Greek-style belt snared a griffin's tail, and then she had to make her way around a multiple-person dragon. Finally she spotted Jake talking to Benny Fields. Jake's usually neat hair was covered by a curly wig and topped by a battered fedora. Benny's ornate turban was surrounded by a cloud of smoke from his ever-present cigar. They both did double takes when they saw her.

"Randi! Wow!" Jake said appreciatively.

Randi grinned. "Hello."

"Hey, where's Dion?"

"I think he left for Morocco. He had an offer that I'm sure he couldn't refuse."

"Oh? Too bad he couldn't be here tonight, though. I wanted to tell him how much I enjoyed working with him."

"I heard everything turned out great," Benny interrupted. "What can you expect? Great cast. Great crew. Great production company. And once we convinced the network execs of that, they laid off our backs too." He took a swig from the Arabic genie bottle Randi had thought was a prop, then shook it. "I'm outta beer. Got to refuel. Be back in a minute," he said, chomping on his cigar.

Jake interrupted her thoughts with a chuckle. "Doesn't he look like something out of *Arabian Nights?*"

"More like something out of an Abbott and Costello movie," Randi said, watching Benny fill his bottle from a keg while his pantaloons bloomed behind him.

"By the way, speaking of Dion—argh!" Jake's hands went to his throat to loosen his long, rainbow-colored scarf after someone stepped on it, almost choking him. "That'll teach me to wear a twenty-foot muffler!"

"Dressing as a time lord does have its drawbacks," Randi said, referring to his Dr. Who disguise.

"Yeah. Listen, before we get separated in the crowd, I have to tell you something about Dion. Remember the gossip and the problems with the network at the beginning of the shoot?"

"I remember." Was Jake going to tell her Dion was guilty after all? Randi wondered with apprehension.

"I thought Dion was responsible, since he's friends with the network's chairman of the board, Bob Savage. The funny thing was, he'd suspected me too." Jake paused and went on. "Then one morning Dion hauled Sally Brown and me into his tent after he heard her gossiping with one of the wranglers. He was determined to find out what was going on. Well, Sally confessed. Boy, was she pathetic! I hate seeing anyone grovel."

"So it was Sally all along," Randi said thoughtfully. "But why?"

"Ambition. Thought she could get places by pandering to the execs. Anyway, Sally cried and said she'd lose her job if you knew. Dion gave her some advice about self-respect and told her she shouldn't be jealous of successful women. She'd need their support if she was ever to become successful herself. Dion and I were both angry, but we agreed to keep her secret until after the shoot as long as she behaved. I thought it only fair that you know now."

"Thanks, Jake. I appreciate your honesty, as always." Randi swallowed hard, wishing she could make up for her doubts about Jake . . . and Dion.

"You know, I thought Dion was a glitzy celebrity at

177

the beginning of the shoot. I ended up being impressed with the guy. I wish I could tell him how I feel."

"I wish I could too."

When Jake's gaze suddenly froze over her shoulder, Randi turned. She blinked hard at what she saw. Had she conjured the image she'd wanted so much to see? Why wasn't he in North Africa? Dion stood at the balcony door, his eyes relentlessly roaming the crowd.

Searching? For her? Randi's heart thudded erratically as she studied the man she loved.

In Grecian splendor, Dion wore a costume framing his perfection. A knee-length chiton was fastened over one shoulder by a large gold brooch. The creamy white material draped both at his waist and hips around a double girdle of soft leather and hammered gold. Most of Dion's chest was bared, as were his hard-muscled legs, which flexed enticingly as he impatiently shifted from one sandaled foot to the other.

The amount of sun-kissed skin he'd left exposed was almost indecent! Randi thought as a rush of warmth blossomed within her.

"I guess I'll get a chance to tell Dion what I thought of him after all," she vaguely heard Jake say. "If I can beat off all the women who seem eager to throw themselves at him, that is."

Suddenly Randi realized there were at least a half-dozen women other than herself drooling over Dion's naked thighs. Then she looked at his face and forgot about everything but rushing into his arms to explain her recent insanity.

Gazes linking, they seemed to be alone, spirits reaching for one another across the crowded room, a haze of love and sensuality already connecting them. Randi moved to

Dion as if in slow motion, her blood thickening, her limbs weakening as if determined to torment her. He, too, seemed frustrated in his attempts to reach her through the milling bodies.

Then the crowd hushed as Olga and Raoul, dressed as two colorful Tibetan gods, descended the winding staircase.

"Welcome to our Halloween festivities celebrating the new year of nature," Olga said, inclining her fanlike headdress. Her long silver earrings tinkled like wind chimes as she moved. "By recognizing the drama of the changing seasons, we can arouse our inner powers."

As a Tibetan Skywalker, her godmother was a celestial vision, Randi thought, tearing her eyes from Dion for a second. Olga's sleeveless panel coat swirled around loose blue pantaloons and silver-booted ankles. Raoul provided a startling contrast in dark blue, swirls of red and gold darting from his compact body like tongues of fire. His mask—that of a demon god—bore the fierce image of a snarling lion baring fangs and tongue.

"Chaos, bad girl!" Olga said indignantly, interrupting her own flow. Chaos was at it again! Randi thought. The audience tittered as the hostess scolded her cat, whose head was swallowed by the spiked punch bowl on the buffet table. "You're going to get drunk again! Shoo!"

Recognizing the authoritative voice, the cat leaped from the table and scurried away.

"I believe the human experience is an inner as well as an outer adventure," Olga calmly continued, lighting the candles. "Take this opportunity to celebrate the changes we can cause within ourselves to make the coming year a better one. Let the festivities begin!"

The room began to swirl with moving color and pulsating sound as Dion stopped in front of Randi.

"I'm sorry," they whispered in unison, but explanations were impossible for the moment.

Caught up in the revelers' dance, they had to be content to link hands and move within a writhing circle of merrymakers. The line stretched throughout the long room and onto the balcony. The dancers did simple steps to the ancient music, weaving in and out of the balcony doors. Finally the drums, flutes and bells were silenced, and the murmur of voices rose.

"I've been doing a lot of thinking since our argument the other day," Dion told her, his expression fierce.

"Yes, well—"· Randi tried to explain.

"Don't interrupt. You're not the director here. This is my scene, and I intend to have my say." Dion glared at her, and Randi held her breath as he continued. "I decided you couldn't help but be suspicious of me, considering the reputation of the Technique."

She began to relax. "You don't understa—"

"I'm not finished." A hoot of laughter interrupted him, and one of Snow White's seven dwarfs came tumbling between them. A look of frustration crossed Dion's face. "Do you think Olga would mind if we found a quiet spot to talk things over upstairs?"

"I've got a better idea. Come on outside," Randi said, taking Dion by the arm and leading him back through the open balcony doors.

Shrieks and splashing sounds made Dion pause, but Randi tugged harder, leading him toward the lantern-lit garden. As they crossed the Chinese bridge, they looked down upon several mermaids, long hair dripping over almost naked breasts. In unison they splashed their fake tails at an older man with blue hair and beard, dressed in gold armor and carrying a trident.

"Look, there's Neptune!" Randi said.

"Not now!" This time it was Dion who did the pulling, almost jerking Randi's arm out of its socket. "It's time we got things settled between us, and you're not finding any more excuses to put it off!"

A happy sound bubbled in Randi's throat, but she shoved it back. Dion was so serious and determined, she didn't want to offend him by laughing.

Grabbing her by the shoulders, he pushed her down onto a stone bench surrounded by flowering rosebushes. With a satisfied smirk, he loomed over her.

"Yes, Dion?"

"As I was saying, I don't blame you for being suspicious of my motives. I did blame you for not facing me with your doubts, but after thinking about it, I guess I can understand that too. Love is such a complicated emotion." He ran a hand through his hair, and Randi noted the gleam of autumn leaves intertwined with the curls. "It makes us do crazy things. Like the other day when I walked away from the car instead of airing everything the way I should have."

"Dion, I realize you—"

"Let me finish!"

"Yes, Dion," Randi said with a meekness that didn't reflect her soaring joy.

"First of all, I have to admit the Technique is a little hard to understand at times. But I want you to know that I used it in my *work* and left it out of our relationship. I am *not* emotionally irresponsible!"

Randi would have agreed with Dion, but he was on a roll, pacing back and forth, earnestly trying to convince

181

her of that which she already knew to be the truth. Obviously he'd geared himself up for this speech. How could she spoil his anticipated victory? Randi decided she'd let Dion "convince" her of his authenticity and love.

"As for my leaving . . ."

A high-pitched giggle came from a comely maiden in a transparent tunic who ran down the path next to the bench, followed closely by a determined-looking satyr. Thinking of what they must be up to, Randi giggled, then sobered when Dion glared at her once more.

". . . I didn't even sign the contracts for *Shifting Sands*," he continued as though he hadn't been interrupted. "When I said I hadn't been discussing anything important with my agent, I didn't know you'd been eavesdropping!"

Randi had the grace to look shamefaced. "I didn't mean to. But why did you lie?" she asked defensively. "I heard enough to know that lead *is* important to you."

"Depends on your perspective," Dion said softly. "It is important to my career, but it's nothing compared to our relationship."

"Did you think I'd stand in your way?"

"I thought you might not be ready to marry me."

"What!" Was this Dion's way of proposing? Randi wondered dazedly.

"Can you blame me for thinking that when I'd just gotten you to admit you loved me? I didn't want to go off and leave you without knowing our relationship was secure. I was trying to hold off making a commitment to the new movie until I could be sure the separation wouldn't end what you and I had, but somehow everything seemed to blow up in my face. I never got a chance to discuss it with you."

"I accept," Randi said suddenly.

"Huh?"

"Did you or did you not ask me to marry you?"

Dion stared, a tremulous smile beginning to curve his lips. "I—I guess I did," he stammered.

"Then I accept," she repeated softly.

Dion seemed dazed as he tangled his fingers in her hair. "You'll really marry me?"

At her happy nod, Dion leaned over to kiss her, gently cupping her cheeks with both hands. It was the sweetest kiss they'd ever shared, Randi thought, feeling as though her heart was about to burst. When he raised his head and removed his hands, she started to protest until she realized he was plucking roses for her. He secured them under the diadem.

"Ah, now you have a golden crown with blazing gems in the shape of red roses, just as Dionysus wove for Ariadne in ancient times."

"And later you'll have to throw them into the heavens, where they'll form a chain of stars," Randi continued lightly, knowing that according to myth, the original Dionysus had so formed the Corona Borealis.

"Shall we be lovers throughout eternity, then, like our namesakes?"

"Are you sure that's how their myth ended?"

"If it isn't, we'll rewrite the script!"

His lips neared hers, but once more they were interrupted.

"Yikes! Beware of wild women!" the same harried satyr warned Dion before running off in the other direction, four scantily clad women now chasing *him*.

Both Randi and Dion burst into laughter. Noting her lover's rueful expression at their lack of privacy, Randi

183

rose and led him to her special place, the red pagoda. If any questions remained unanswered, she would ask them later. Now it was important to Randi that she give Dion the gift of her trust.

"We're going to be alone to celebrate!" she insisted, locking the door behind them.

"Celebrate? Or consummate?"

"Is there a difference when lovers are involved?" she asked, her throaty laugh filled with expectation as she shuttered the windows closest to the path outside.

Once assured of their privacy, Randi loosened and dropped her decorative girdle onto one of the cushioned benches. Then, knowing her lover closely watched her every movement, she began to undo the few hooks she had fastened on her costume.

Dion stood framed by the screened back window, which overlooked a small drop. Moonlight washed through his hair and over his shoulders, its silvery beams catching and melting with glints of gold, dazzling Randi, making her see him as the mythical Dionysus, golden god of ecstasy. Suddenly her hands shook with the intensity of her desire-filled love. Randi swallowed hard and forced herself to concentrate on the task of removing her clothing.

"Why do I get the feeling that I didn't have to try quite so hard to convince you of my honorable intentions?" Dion asked breathlessly.

Not answering immediately, Randi smiled at his accurate intuition. Unable to see Dion's face, she felt his eyes glued to her full breasts and their tightening nipples as she allowed the chiton to form a puddle around her feet. Her pale skin glowed, set aflame in silver by the full moon. Quickly she stripped the flesh-colored bikinis, leaving only her jewelry and the sweet-smelling roses to costume her.

"Do you mind that I'd already decided I'd been wrong?" she finally asked as heat throbbed through her, assuring Randi she was ready for a joyful reunion. "I couldn't bear to stop your flow of beautiful words."

Randi crossed to Dion as he released the double girdle that held his skimpy costume intact. She trailed her fingers across his warm, very mortal shoulder and thrilled when the material gave way before her hand. She heard it whisper its way to the floor of the pagoda. Splaying her fingers across his chest, she trailed them down his stomach, marveling at how the smooth flesh hardened into muscle at the slightest contact. *This* golden god was earthbound, hers to adore and touch, Randi thought with satisfaction as she helped him strip completely. Then she stroked Dion intimately, treasuring the life force that leaped to response.

"Ariadne, my beautiful goddess, you've made me feel things that I don't want to lose."

"You'll never lose me," she predicted as his thumbs drew circles around the points of her breasts. "Nor I you."

Turning her in to his embrace, Dion kissed her lingeringly. Eyes open, Randi watched his face, half glowing by moonlight, half shadowed in darkness. The imagery made her think of the way she saw the inner Dion. Although he'd revealed so much of himself, there were the shadowed places and secrets in his heart. That nebulous half of his inner self had to be taken on trust, yet she knew it would be worthwhile, as surely as she knew the darkened half of Dion's face was as beautiful as the half lit by the moon.

"I love you, Dion," she whispered, thrilled when the words were echoed quickly.

Scattered cushions across the floor provided a makeshift bed as they lay together. Dion stroked and caressed every part of her until Randi thought she would go mad with wanting. He filled her with his fingers, stroked her with his tongue, but it was only when she was panting and crying out his name that Dion pulled her to him. Both on their sides, their bodies touched from lips to toes.

"This is the way I want us to be always," Dion murmured. "Equal partners in life, side by side forever."

Arching closer, Randi knew blessed relief when she felt him slide against her thigh and into her. Closing her eyes, she nibbled at Dion's neck, savoring the salty taste she captured in her love bites. She drew in his scent, strong with his wanting her.

She let him take her to places where gods dwelled, all bright light and harmony. Then their bodies fused and flamed out into the night, where they were dusted by the stars and bathed by the moon before floating down gently, earthbound mortals once more.

"Didn't I tell you how it was, Foxy? We *are* poetry together," Dion whispered after kissing her.

"There's that line again," Randi said, but this time there was no distrust coloring her tone, and she took pleasure in their still-joined bodies.

"That's another thing I meant to clear up," Dion told her, the side of his head resting against his upper arm. With one finger, he traced Randi's cheekbone. "I added that line to *Distant Lightning*."

"Ad lib?"

"Uh-huh. My romantic streak was showing, I guess,

186

and the director liked it, so he left it in. I think a relationship *can* be like poetry. Two people can stand alone, just as individual words can. But joined, they complement each other and can flow to new dimensions, like lines in a poem. I want us to flow together."

"We will." Randi kissed his fingers and turned onto her back. As her gaze flicked over the familiar dark blue interior of her childhood haunt, its intricate moldings hidden by the darkness, she smiled.

"What's that beautiful smile for?"

"I was thinking how this pagoda has always brought me luck," Randi said, shivering as Dion's fingers traced patterns on her flattened breasts. "Olga's magic pagoda. Ever since I can remember I've come here to daydream and make wishes, so many of which have come true. Even as a child, I wanted to be a director of quality films. With *Chrysalis*, I got what I thought was my most important wish, but then a few days ago, when I thought our love had been an illusion, I realized it wasn't enough. What good was having a dream come true if I didn't have someone special with whom I could share it? Having a loving, supportive partner is equally important."

"Now the romantic in *you* is showing," Dion teased, kissing her on the tip of the nose.

"M-m-m. And now my dream is complete. Even when I knew I was wrong about my assumptions, I wasn't sure it would happen," Randi admitted. "I thought we were star-crossed lovers."

"No way. I knew you were right for me the first day you gave me a hard time three years ago. And when I realized you were interested in me, I knew our love would be star-blessed."

"You did?"

187

"Uh-huh. It just took us longer than some to realize it. Look at Olga's story. Doesn't that prove we were destined for each other? When I sat and considered what you said about our relationship mirroring Shann and Lara's, it blew my mind. It was almost spooky!"

"You never saw the connections until I brought them up?"

"Afraid not. I guess I'm just not as clever as you. I wonder what Olga will make of it."

"Don't you dare tell her!"

"Why not?"

"Because my godmother thinks she knows everything! She walks around spouting predictions like some seer. No doubt she'll take credit for our romance and tell everyone she planned it from the start!"

"Maybe she did," Dion said thoughtfully. "When did she write *Chrysalis,* anyway?"

"Oh, I think she started it about three years ago. . . ." Randi's voice trailed off as she realized it had been right after her first short-lived affair with Dion. "No, that's ridiculous." But Randi winced, knowing if it was true, they'd never hear the end of it! Randi turned back to Dion and tilted her head toward the open window and the clear dark sky beyond. "I'd rather believe our love was written in the stars."

"And so it is," Dion agreed before sealing that thought with a kiss.

All-new Candlelight Newsletter

An exceptional, *free* offer awaits readers of Dell's incomparable Candlelight Ecstasy and Supreme Romances.

Subscribe to our all-new CANDLELIGHT NEWSLETTER and you will receive—at absolutely no cost to you—exciting, exclusive information about today's finest romance novels and novelists. You'll be part of a select group to receive sneak previews of upcoming Candlelight Romances, well in advance of publication.

You'll also go behind the scenes to "meet" our Ecstasy and Supreme authors, learning firsthand where they get their ideas and how they made it to the top. News of author appearances and events will be detailed, as well. And contributions from the Candlelight editor will give you the inside scoop on how she makes her decisions about what to publish—and how *you* can try your hand at writing an Ecstasy or Supreme.

You'll find all this and more in Dell's CANDLELIGHT NEWSLETTER. And best of all, *it costs you nothing*. That's right! It's Dell's way of thanking our loyal Candlelight readers and of adding another dimension to your reading enjoyment.

Just fill out the coupon below, return it to us, and look forward to receiving the first of many CANDLELIGHT NEWSLETTERS—overflowing with the kind of excitement that only enhances our romances!

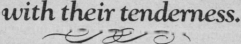

Candlelight
Ecstasy Romances™

$1.95 each